SHIELD

NAMELESS SOULS MC
BOOK 4

EVIE MITCHELL

THUNDER THIGHS PUBLISHING

DEDICATION

To my Greedy Reader group
It's been a hot minute since we ventured to the end of the world,
but I adore that you're frothing for more biker badness!

And to my husband.
Always.

ACKNOWLEDGEMENT OF COUNTRY

I acknowledge the Traditional Custodians of the lands on which I write, the Ngunnawal people, and pay my respect to elders both past and present.

I acknowledge the continued and deep spiritual relationship of the Australian Aboriginal and Torres Strait Islander peoples' to this land, and their unique cultural and spiritual relationships to the land, waters and seas and their rich contribution to society.

Always was, always will be.

CONTENT WARNINGS

Please note the following content warnings include
SPOILERS for this book.

SPOILERS BELOW

Theme triggers

This is book 4 in the Nameless Souls MC series. It begins at the end of modern timelines and features references to a virus that caused the world to descend into an apocalyptic state.

Medical triggers

This story contains references to terminal cancer, death of relatives, and associated grief. References to deceased, dead bodies and killing. The story includes descriptions of injuries. The story includes references to a virus resulting in lockdowns, quarantines, illness, and death.

Relationship triggers

It also features references to lost family and missing friends.

Sexual triggers

The story features graphic sex scenes, including consensual choking, oral sex, public sex, praise kink, breeding kink, and dirty talk. The main characters engage in spontaneous sex and do not use a condom. However, the female main character is on birth control.

More information

If you have any concerns with the depictions in this story or would like further information before reading, please email EvieMitchellAuthor@gmail.com

END SPOILERS

SHIELD

Shield

As President of the Nameless Souls, it's my responsibility to see my Club through the darkest of nights.

Then the darkest night arrived. Our world ended.

The disease tore through our Club, taking friends and family. But we held on to hope, fighting for our future.

It's my duty to protect my people. It's my honour to bleed for my Club.

Then I met her—the woman who rips out my fucking heart.

I'd die for her.

But sometimes you can't protect someone from the true demon—themself.

THE STORY SO FAR

Day 651 - Post the Dark

Society's collapse was foreseeable.

It's a pity no one listened to me.

Overcrowding, misinformation, disinformation, declining government trust, a fraudulent capitalist system, climate change, resource scarcity, and global power tensions—each of these things could have led to a total implosion.

But my computer program and I predicted the pandemic. A virus that would race across the world, spreading through high-density areas and rapidly overtaking any government's ability to halt the spread.

For three years, I'd battled professors, bureaucrats, and government departments to be heard. I'd sent detailed reports. I'd explained in stunning detail the trajectory and what needed to happen to slow the spread.

Do you think the old white guys listened to me—a young, attractive, intelligent female, Vietnamese-Australia from an immigrant family?

Hell no.

Then Scenario 587 came true. The virus had emerged in the United States, quickly ravaging the world. It targeted anyone with an X chromosome—which meant everyone. But women and those with additional chromosomes were hardest hit.

The virus's reinfection rate was less than 2%. One and done might sound like a blessing, but most who contracted it ended up dead. In a matter of weeks, the death toll reached in the millions. Within a year, it had escalated to the billions.

Knowing this would happen, I'd planned for it. I'd planned for every scenario and considered every option.

Enter - Operation Redlight

But planning for a pandemic and living through it are two very different things.

Myself and twelve other women had hunkered down at our university, determined to survive the apocalypse. Hand-picked for their skills—we'd had all the knowledge and support necessary to live through this world-ending event.

I'd smugly assumed we were safe. Isolated from the rest of society in a remote area. I'd calculated our rate of survival in the high seventies.

I'd failed to account for the unexpected.

In what appeared to be a synchronised effort, governments worldwide had destroyed communications. Satellites were blown from the skies, communications cut, all signals jammed.

The world had gone dark, silent and still. Overnight my data sources dried up, leaving us to fend for ourselves.

I'd predicted militia, cannibals, rebels, even radicalised arms of the government. I hadn't anticipated the zombies.

Known as 'bastards', these mutated humans weren't true versions of the walking dead. They lived, their minds destroyed and bodies ravaged by whatever infection had taken hold. Gnarled, clawed hands, gnashing teeth, and a desire to rip and tear anything and anyone who had the misfortune to cross their path.

Like something out of a horror movie, they prowled in packs called Hordes. Spread across hundreds of kilometres of hunting grounds, their numbers growing larger even as they became increasingly desperate for new food sources.

Their feeding grounds reportedly stretched from far north Queensland down to central New South Wales. But as survivor numbers dwindled due to starvation, infighting, Horde attacks and poor medical care—the bastards were beginning to migrate in search of new food sources.

And it was that migration that had pushed The Purge—a militia group—into our haven a full two years ahead of schedule. We'd had time to consolidate our holdings, but we weren't trained enough at this point to do more than return fire.

We'd survived our first brush with The Purge by the skin of our teeth, but not without injury and losses. When it was all done, two of our women were missing—Jules and Lilith.

The Purge had been a wake-up call. With our survival statistics rapidly falling, we'd been forced to align ourselves with other survivors.

The Nameless Souls Motorcycle Club had embraced us with open arms, their need for people with our skills was welcomed.

The fact they needed women also wasn't lost on us.

Ellie—our biochemist—designed a way to mass-produce biofuel. In a world where fuel is a precious commodity, her brain is more valuable than water.

Don't worry, I'm just as valuable. I created my own telecommunications network.

And now we're travelling to the remaining two chapters of the Nameless Souls MC. Our plan is to teach them how to create their own biofuel and connect them via my network.

It's dangerous. It's deadly.

And stats say it's our only option for long-term survival.

I don't believe in God, but if anyone reading this does, now would be the time to pray.

— Audrey

1

AUDREY

This is a stupid idea.

I watched Ava and Lottie embrace, the sisters as different as two people could be. Ava, with her rough edges, sharp points and biting sarcasm, contrasted with her soft, comforting sister. Their hair said a lot about them, with Lottie's riot of fizzy curls projecting a wild but soft vibe, while Ava's short hair was pulled into a strict, no-nonsense braid.

They shouldn't be separated.

In the Before, Ava had been a Major in the army—and those skills had come in handy as society disintegrated into a post-apocalyptic wreck.

Charlotte—or as we called her, Lottie—not so much. A veterinarian with a tender touch, I'd seen her soft heart break more than once since the world had ended.

"Don't worry," I heard Ava reassure Lottie. "These bastards have nothing on me."

"It's not the bastards I'm worried about," Lottie retorted, holding her sister tight. "It's the idiots with guns. I just— promise you'll come back?"

Ava squeezed her tight. "Promise. You won't even notice I'm gone."

A lump formed in my throat, my chest contracting as I watched the two women.

This is why I don't do family.

I cleared my throat, interrupting their moment. "I'm out."

I shook my head, my straight black hair whipping in the strong breeze. Tucking it absently behind my ear, I nodded at the mad woman. "Ava, good luck. Don't get killed, or I'll find a way to clone you and kill you again."

She grinned. "I don't doubt it." Stepping close, she surprised me by wrapping an arm around me, offering a hug.

Ava wasn't the hugging type, nor was I—usually. Her arms felt warm and solid, comforting even as I stiffened, feeling awkward by this non-Ava-esq display of affection.

Unsure, I returned her embrace, giving her a quick squeeze.

Are we huggers now? Or is she seeking reassurance that she's made the right decision?

She pulled back, her normally stern gaze softened with amusement. "Don't run into any trouble while I'm gone. And be nice to Pope, he can't help being a doofus."

I forced a grin. "No promises."

I watched Ava farewell the other members of our small tribe, her expression shuttering as she turned toward the waiting vehicle.

This is it. We're divided once more.

There'd been thirteen of us when we first began back at the College. Thirteen resilient, strong, intelligent women with the kind of skills you needed to survive.

Thirteen displaced women searching for belonging.

I'd recruited them, taking them in and purposefully

cultivating a sense of family and inclusion in order to keep them in our small bubble. Our safety had been contingent on each of us working together in harmony. I'd calculated the risks based on numerous factors, including connection, personality and skills, before inviting and accepting each one.

I hadn't anticipated forming my own connections. It was incredibly inconvenient to realise that I was coming to rely upon these women for more than their survival skills.

Feelings are simply chemical responses to stimuli. Connection is nothing more than a feeling invoked by a cocktail of serotonin, dopamine and oxytocin. Rise above it, Audrey. It's the only way to survive.

Lottie wrapped an arm around my waist, holding me against her. "What are her actual chances of finding Jules and Lilith alive?"

I knew she wanted reassurance, but I had none to offer.

"Low."

As low as her chances of returning unscathed.

Despite her skills, and that of the man she was travelling with, I didn't hold out much hope for her finding Lilith and Jules, let alone her returning in one piece.

For one, she and Ghost were travelling directly toward a highly populated area that was no doubt filled with starving, displaced, distrustful people. They might have both been trained in combat, but two people against an entire town? It didn't make for good odds.

Then add to that the fact she was female, and we'd somehow been reduced to a breedable commodity since the whole end-of-the-world bullshit had happened. And add to *that*, Jules and Lilith had been missing for weeks without any evidence they were even still alive.

Well, let's just say none of it added to the positive outcome equation.

It burned to admit it because in the Before, Jules and Lilith had been some of my best friends. When I'd formed my end-of-the-world plan, Ellie, Jules and Lilith had been the first I'd asked to join—and from there, we'd found the rest of our motley crew.

And now look at us. Divided, separated, lost.

I refused to contemplate the demise of my missing friends.

"I believe in her," Lottie whispered as Ghost started the SUV, the engine purring loudly in the quiet of the court-yard. "I think she'll find them and bring them home."

And where exactly is home?

I nodded, having learned enough in the past few years to recognise when someone wanted me to lie to them.

"I believe you. If anyone can do it, Ava can."

The SUV pulled out, bouncing down the long dirt and gravel track before it disappeared into the brush surrounding the property. Slowly the giant doors to the fort-like wall surrounding the farm closed, sealing us back in.

Lottie sighed heavily, leaning her head on my shoulder. "And then there were five."

I snorted, turning us back toward the farmhouse. "There are a lot more of us than that."

"You don't think it feels a little like we're slowly being picked off?"

"No," I lied. "It feels like we're doing side quests."

It was her turn to snort. "Like this is some kind of *Dungeon and Dragon* game?"

"Something like that." I paused, catching sight of Ella and Runner across the way. They were locked in a passionate embrace, her back pressed against the giant wall, his hands all over her as they kissed, uncaring of the attention they may attract.

"I see they're at it again."

I glanced to my left to find Jo standing beside me, her arms crossed over her chest. Her short hair brushed her cheeks, her normally serious face lightened by a small, amused smile.

A talented mechanic, she'd come to us via her two younger sisters who she'd been supporting through college. At first, I'd been hesitant to invite her into our small community, worried her rough edges and sarcastic gruffness would cause friction within our ranks. But I'd quickly learned that she viewed the world with a pragmaticism coupled with a fiercely protective need to defend those she considered close.

At some point, I'd apparently become someone she loved. It was a strange thing to realise that her fondness extended to me.

"I'm jealous," I admitted. "Since I left the vibrators back at Adaminaby, I've been in rather desperate need."

Jo pressed her lips together, her throat bopping as she swallowed. On my other side, Lottie tossed back her head, her laughter tumbling out free before it was caught by the wind and swept away.

I'd never understood why telling the truth about your feelings or needs inspired such merriment in others.

"A grave issue indeed," Jo said, her lips quirked. "Are fingers not good enough?"

I sighed heavily. "I've never been able to just flick my bean."

Lottie burst into another round of giggles which Jo and I ignored.

"No?" She tilted her head to one side. "Why?"

I tapped my temple with my knuckles. "Too many thoughts."

"Ah." Jo nodded sagely. "I understand."

"You do?"

"Of course. An orgasm is as much about the brain as it is about the nerve endings."

I shook my head. "Not when I'm using the rose vibrator, it's not."

Lottie doubled over, her laughter drawing far too much attention.

I assumed she was laughing at me, but I never quite knew what I said that drew such a reaction from people. Feeling like a piece that didn't quite fit, I began to walk away. Jo fell into step beside me, her hands tucked into grease and dirt-streaked overalls.

At least she rarely laughs at me.

"What are you gonna do about it?"

"Find a man."

Her eyebrow lifted. "Oh really? Which one? Pope?"

I laughed. "No, of course not. That man whore could be crawling with diseases. No," I decided, glancing up at the sky. "When we move on from here, I'll ask the first man I meet for his sexual history. If it is acceptable—and I find him attractive—then I'll sleep with him."

I felt Jo's gaze on me as we headed toward the big barn on the far side of the property.

"You're serious, aren't you?"

"Oh yes," I agreed cheerfully. "I think so much better after sex. During my dissertation, I hired a male escort." I made a face. "He was terrible. I had to train him. He ended up giving me money back."

Jo stumbled, then righted herself. "An escort?"

"Yes. No orgasms, though. But I know it'll happen one day."

Jo cocked an eyebrow. "No orgasms?"

I shook my head. "He'd been...." I sighed, closing my eyes as I remembered Jared's big body. "Strong. Large. Enthusiastic. He was a wonderfully physical lover, but my goodness, he didn't know a clitoris from a belly button."

Jo snorted. "I believe that challenge afflicts most men."

I nodded sagely. "I agree."

We walked on quietly for a beat.

"But no orgasms with just him or...?" she asked.

"In general." I shrugged. "A mechanically assisted orgasm appears to be my only option. But sex itself is very pleasurable. I assume that when—if—it happens, it will be very satisfying."

"Because men are useless?"

"In part. But also because of this." I tapped the side of my head. "Physical exertion brings me clarity. It is virtually impossible for me to quiet my thoughts."

Jo nodded. "So why an escort and not a fuck buddy or a boyfriend?"

Because they expect some level of commitment.

I swallowed. "I don't need a man whose ego I have to pander to in my life. Escorts are transactional. And while Jared was ever so pretty—he even shaved his genitals—he was conveniently disposed of."

Jo coughed, then coughed again before changing the subject. "And on that note, when are we leaving?"

I glanced at the sky, observing the cloud formations, wind and temperature variations.

"Tomorrow," I decided. "Cunnamulla awaits."

2

SHIELD

So, this is how I die.

I watched the bastards swarm my motorcycle, my heart breaking as I watched my painstakingly restored pride and joy disappear under a crush of bodies.

Not that she's much use these days.

I stood on the hot tin roof of the toilet block, watching the horde gnash their teeth and scratch at the flimsy tin walls—their mindless rage capable of fuelling them for hours.

Will death come from exposure or dehydration? From a rogue bastard bite? Or will I get lucky and just suffer a sudden onset heart attack from which I never awaken?

I pulled the gun from my hip, checking the chamber.

"Fuck."

I had five bullets left, zero water, and a horde of about fifty bastards blocking my escape.

Stupid fuck. Should have abandoned her.

I watched, my heart heavy, as another bastard tripped over my bike, dragging her across the gravel, shredding her paint job.

"We had a good run, darling." I lowered my head, closing my eyes as I mourned both of us.

Here lies Rusty and Shield, killed by a horde because the fucker decided his bike meant more than his life.

I fancied that I could hear her growling in the distance, her ghost coming to welcome me home.

My head raised, ears pricking.

"What the fuck?"

Those weren't Rusty's pipes. Either I was hallucinating, or those were actual motorcycle engines.

Shit. Cannibal, militia, or friend?

I palmed my gun, considering my options.

"Let's see, a horde of brainless bastards ready to rip me apart?"

As if on cue, a bastard smashed into the side of the toilet block, the metal buckling under his weight.

"Or rescue with the potential for a long slow torturous death followed by a roasting over an open flame?"

I raised my pistol. "Well, this is an easy fucking decision."

With practised ease, I shot twice, taking out two bastards in the process.

The engines drew closer, their roar music to my ears.

The bastards grew restless, twisting and turning, bodies shaking as their primal minds attempted to decide whether to fight or flee.

Go on, fuckers. You know you want to.

Half the horde ran, taking off into the bush behind the toilet block. The other half remained, advancing on the road.

The vehicles finally appeared over the ridge, shining beacons of mechanical hope.

Two tankers, an SUV, and three bikes. Well, if this isn't a Mad Max movie waiting to happen, I don't know what is.

I grinned as I clocked one of the bikes at the front of the pack.

"I'll be fucking damned."

I lifted a hand as the party flew down the highway, the front bike's light flashing in acknowledgement.

The bikes dropped back, allowing the trucks to glide forward as the remaining bastards swarmed the road. The front tanker hit the horde at speed, taking out half of the pack. The second tanker followed, cleaning up most of the remaining swarm.

I winced, listening to the unholy crunch of bodies under wheels. "That's effective."

I crossed my arms, frowning as a woman I didn't recognise leaned out the front passenger window of one of the SUVs. Her black hair flew behind her as she laid waste to the remaining bastards, the machine gun in her hands tearing rotten limbs from bone.

With a flourish, the SUV skidded to a halt in front of the toilet block, the woman tilting her head back to grin up at me.

Her large eyes were wide and shining with friendly amusement behind her thick-rimmed precariously balanced glasses. Her limbs were long and graceful and kissed a golden pink by the warm sun. A gush of wind caught the loose strands of her straight ebony hair, tossing the tresses across her face.

She swiped impatiently at her face, brushing them away.

"Hey," she said, shoving glasses up her nose. "I'm Audrey. Looks like you need a rescue."

My gaze swept down her top. The material hung open, granting me an unobstructed view of her tits. My cock hardened in response.

Oh, darlin'. I'm not the one who needs a rescue.

A lazy smile pulled at my lips.

"You could say that."

A bastard tumbled out of the dense brush behind the toilet block, gnashing its teeth as it ran at the vehicle. A dog leapt at the back window of the SUV, barking furiously. Casually, Audrey pushed her glasses up her nose, raised her gun and shot it in the head.

I watched it fall, twitch once and die.

Shit. I think I'm in love.

"If you want to get out of here, you better climb down," she said, lowering her weapon without so much as a flinch. "We're on a tight schedule." She pretended to look at a non-existent watch on her wrist. "Need to get to Tindarey by nightfall." She jerked her finger to the SUV. "You can ride with Killer."

"Killer?"

She grinned. "The name is well deserved, trust me."

I jumped from my perch as the motorcycles circled and the trucks parked. Dusting my hands on my equally filthy jeans, I shook my head, grinning when I recognised my rescue party.

In addition to the pretty Audrey, there were my Club members—Runner, Pope, and Wrath.

What are the chances?

Runner, a tall, lean brother from the Adaminaby chapter, reached out to grasp my hand, hauling me in for a back-slapping hug.

"Prez," he greeted with a laugh. "What the fuck are you doing out here?"

"Could ask the same of you." I released him and turned to Pope, getting the same welcome. "Grateful you motherfuckers arrived at the just right time. Was getting mighty hot up there."

Pope's grin came quick and easy. "That's what she said."

I shove him away, chuckling.

The guy was younger than the rest of us, somewhere in his late twenties, with the kind of rockstar looks that landed him a lot of pussy. Could've gone to his head, could have made him a dick, but while the guy took what was offered, word was he gave just as much back.

As much as it killed me to collect this kind of info about the brothers in my Club, it was my job to know it. I ran a tight ship. The brothers could party, they could get wild, fuck around, do whatever might not have been considered entirely legal in the Before. But there was a code of honour. I'd learned the hard way that men who were dicks to women, kids or animals tended to be the ones who stabbed you when your back was turned.

It was one of the reasons I was headed to Adaminaby.

Pope stepped back, and Wrath took his place, clasping one of my hands, his gaze searching my face.

Wrath had been nomad since just before the Dark— when the world that was already shit had truly gone to hell. Bombs dropping, communications broken, militia, the army, fuckwits... it had been a truly fucked period and remained so. With no comms, we'd been forced to rely on nomads like Wrath—talented soldiers who knew how to ride, fight and live rough. They did it. They ate the danger; they lived with the fear and loneliness—all for their brothers, for the Club. They did it to make sure our people had the information we needed to be safe.

I needed them, but fuck if I didn't hate forcing them onto a path I wasn't sure they'd emerge from.

I looked Wrath over, noting the new salt and pepper at his temples and worry lines at the corners of his eyes. He had a leanness to him—no doubt brought on by a lack of decent meals. But overall, the brother looked good, healthy and—dare I say—content?

"You good?" he asked, voice low.

I gave him a chin lift. "You?"

Colour me shook; the fucker actually smiled.

"Yeah."

"Jesus," I muttered, stepping back and slapping a hand to my chest. "Someone broke Wrath."

"Nah," Runner drawled, unclipping his water canister from his waist to toss it to me. "He found a girl who put him back together."

My eyebrows lifted. "A girl or *the* girl?"

Wrath crossed his arms, planting his feet. "Old lady."

I knew what that meant—he wouldn't be going nomad anymore. It'd be a loss for the Club, but I was glad he'd found a little peace in the chaos.

I nodded, accepting his declaration. "Happy for you, brother."

"It's Kate."

I frowned, not comprehending his declaration before realisation slammed into me.

"As in—?"

He nodded.

"Well fuck." I huffed out an amused laugh. "Thought she was gone to the wind?"

Wrath's lips twisted up. "Seems the wind thought kindly enough of us to bring her back."

I scratched my chin, my mind racing. "She's a plant girl, right? Was doing something with plants?"

"B-b-b-botanist," came the stumbled reply.

I twisted, surprised to see a group of women approaching from one of the vehicles.

Women.

The virus's rampage had depleted the world's population. In the blink of an eye, families were torn apart, friends dead. Females were particularly hard hit. The scientists in the Before had explained the virus did something with the X chromosome—meaning men, while vulnerable, at least had a 50-50 chance. Women and those with chromosomal abnormalities? Not so much.

Two percent. That had been the survival rate before the world went dark. Two fucking percent.

There'd been promise of a vaccine. The government had started rolling it out, then the world went to shit.

"Fuck," I muttered, watching the women stroll toward me. "Where'd you find them?"

"They found us."

I glanced at Runner, finding him watching me. "You claimed one?"

He grinned. "Of course. And she's a fucking biochemist." His arm swept out to encompass the oil tankers. "Fuel, brother. She can conjure fuel."

Fuck.

With a skill like that, the woman was more precious than the fucking air we breathed.

And just as valuable to every other motherfucker in this godforsaken world.

As if on cue, his woman moved to his side, pressing into him in a half hug. Runner's arm automatically wrapped around her, holding her to him.

"Prez, this is Ellie."

Blonde hair, big tits, curves. She was exactly Runner's type.

I held out a hand for her to shake. "Pleasure, darlin'."

She took my hand, tilting her head to one side as she read the patch on my kutte.

"Prez?" she asked.

"National President, baby girl," Runner explained, his arm clasped around his woman. "Actual name is Shield. He's who you have to thank for us having half a fighting chance. Called our separation from society early, ordered the chapters to amalgamate, stockpile, weaponize."

Not early enough.

"I hear you're who I have to thank for this abundance?" I swept a hand to encompass tankers.

She dipped her head, a blush touching her cheeks. "It was a joint effort."

I glanced at Wrath, unsurprised to find him in a similar clinch with his woman.

Strawberry blonde hair, startling blue eyes, and a body that reminded me of pin-up girls even when filthy and cased in utilitarian clothing, Kate had always been a looker. Just as I and every other fucker in the Club had known she'd always been Wrath's.

"Shield, you remember Kate?" Wrath guided them both forward with a hand to his woman's lower back.

"Absolutely," I took her hand, giving her a warm squeeze. "Great to see you again."

"You too."

"Your pa still running Adaminaby?"

The jovial atmosphere cracked, tension shimmering around us.

"No," Kate whispered, her face hardening. "He's d-dead."

My shoulders eased. "Good."

Her mouth dropped open, her eyebrows rising. "Good?"

I nodded, crossing my arms over my chest. "If he wasn't, I'd be seeing to it myself. Old Prez fucked up putting him in charge."

Wrath rubbed his chin. "Why do you say that?"

Anger bubbled my blood.

"Men at the Plantation raided a Purge safehouse. The fuckers were running drugs through our area, fucking up the local populace and decimating what was left of the community we're working to preserve."

I caught the women exchanging knowing looks.

"They had women. Lots of 'em. Selling 'em, using 'em. Filthy, starving, desperate."

The image of that hot box with women barely alive, filthy, traumatised—it would stay with me forever.

"Cleaned shop. Got the women back to the Plantation. Got them help. They're Club now. Those that wanted to stay. The rest, we did what we could to make them safe."

Some hadn't made it. Too far gone in the head or their body. Others had decided to make their own way. But those that had stayed had begun making their home with us. Some had men, some women, some alone or with friends they'd begun to make. They were putting down roots and making their lives amongst my people.

They were my people now. And I had to protect them. All of them.

"What does 'clean shop' mean?" Audrey asked from her place behind Kate.

I softened my voice. "Killed them, darlin'."

She nodded, shoving her glasses up her nose. "Good."

Amused, I crossed my arms, locking eyes with her. "You condone violence?"

"When it is deserved." She threw her arms out to encompass the world around us. "And I can't see a police officer or judge anywhere."

I raised an eyebrow, impressed by her pragmatism. I'd travelled through rugged country over the last three years, each time forced to choose my life over another's. I took in her gaze, noting the shadows that played behind her eyes.

These violent delights have violent ends.

"W-w-what happened then?" Kate asked, drawing my gaze back to her. I noted the tension in her shoulders, the way her lips puckered at the corners, and her skin pinched under her eyes.

She knows.

I softened my tone, watching her reaction. "One was Nameless Souls. Had been brought up from Kiama and stayed in Adaminaby until Gus and his woman summoned her. Next thing, she woke up in a truck bound with another girl."

"He handed them to the Purge."

I nodded. "Gift-fucking-wrapped." My hands curled into fists. "Our Club does a lot of shit to survive—kill, steal, deal. But never—and I mean fucking *never*—will we resort to selling our people for safety."

Kate's tension eased, her head nodding. "Agree."

Wrath moved then, his arm tightening around his woman. "Kate took care of it. Gus is gone."

I eyed Kate, noting the new edge to her. "Appreciate it, Kate. Sorry you have to wear that mark on your soul."

She shook her head. "I wear nothing. The man didn't deserve to breathe. All I did was scrub the scum away."

I wanted to ask further questions, but her gaze cut to Wrath, and I saw the emotion simmering under the surface. For all she talked a good talk, the woman had demons.

And yet, she hadn't stuttered when delivering her verdict. Interesting.

"Who took lead?" I asked, changing the subject.

"Brothers voted. Hazard's up."

My eyebrows rose, a grin creeping across my face. "And he accepted?"

"We didn't exactly give him any choice."

I chuckled, imagining his reaction. "That must have been a sight."

"Let's just say leadership isn't his preferred position, but he's settling in."

I bet.

Hazard was a good choice. Reliable, trustworthy, knew how to calm tensions and when to escalate. He dealt with shit swiftly, held his head in a jam, and was strategic— always two steps ahead of the rest of the Club.

Tension I'd been carrying for months loosened in my gut. I should have trusted that the Club would take care of business.

I glanced at the women hanging behind our small group.

"And they are?"

Runner gestured them forward.

"This is Jo and Audrey."

I shook hands with Jo, noting the suspicious gleam in her eyes and the proud tilt of her head. An inch or two above average height, the woman was broad and strong with plain brunette hair just long enough to tie into a short braid. Her dark skin held a smattering of freckles and a touch of red from the sun. She exuded 'fuck off' vibes, her manner coarse, her expression closed.

I liked her immediately.

Jo struck me as the kind of woman you didn't mess with unless you were ready to dig deep and uncover the numerous secrets hiding behind those sad, suspicious eyes.

"Pleasure," I murmured, letting her hand go. "How'd you get mixed up with this lot?"

The woman's lips tipped up into a grudging smile. "Not through any choice of mine, I can assure you."

I chuckled, turning to the last of the group—and the woman who intrigued me most.

"Audrey," she said, sticking out her hand. "But we've already met."

"That we have." I slid my palm against hers, surprised to find her skin a silk and callous combination.

Not just a pretty face.

Her glasses were big on her small face, emphasising her golden eyes. Her inky black hair had been pulled back into a high ponytail, strands slipping free to fall around her face. In one word—stunning. I had a feeling she could bring a man to his knees.

No complaints here.

As if hearing my thoughts, Audrey's lips tipped up.

"You're attractive," she told me, her gaze roaming over my face. "Pity about the beard."

I raised a hand to stroke the offensive facial hair. "My beard is a problem?"

She nodded. "I can't tell if you have a weak chin. A woman wants to ride a man's face, not fall off due to lack of depth and jaw strength."

Behind me, I heard poorly smothered laughter and a sigh of exasperation.

"That happen often?" I asked, swallowing my amusement.

She sighed heavily. "More often than you think. It's enough to make you reconsider oral sex."

Unable to resist the devil sitting on my shoulder, I stepped closer, dropping my voice.

"Baby, if you're that desperate, I'll shave."

She blinked once, her expression morphing into pure delight. "Seriously?"

I grinned, stupidly pleased that I'd surprised her.

You wanna cool it? You got a job to do. She may be cute as fuck, but you can't be fucking around while your people are in need.

"Absolutely," I answered, ignoring my conscious.

She clasped her hands together in front of her, dancing from foot to foot. "When? Now? Can we—"

"Heads up," Runner interrupted. "Company."

Jolted from the pleasure of Audrey, I glanced up, noting the movement on the far horizon.

"That'll be the migration."

"Migration?" Pope asked, shooting me a look.

"Between here and Cobar is a shit fight. Purge, refugees, and bastards flowing from one end of the highway to the other and on every road in between." I shook my head. "Nearly got gunned down for my bike."

"Refugees?" Pope asked, his eyebrows raising.

I nodded once, my lips curling in distaste. "Brisbane through Sydney is a mess. Government bombed whatever they could to try and stop the flow of bastards. Failed. Big time. People have been running out of those areas for months, following the main highways trying to find a place to settle."

"Which in turn is making them feeding grounds for bastards," Wrath finished, his expression knowing.

"It's gotten worse since winter," I confirmed. "If we're headed to Cunnamulla, our best bet is to go back roads, which means avoiding Cobar and Burke."

Pope's eyebrows rose. "You're suggesting we loop out to Sturt?"

I nodded. "It'll add days to our trip, but—"

"It'll be safer," Wrath finished, nodding once. "If it was just us and the tankers, I might suggest we risk going forward. But with the women...." He let his thought trail off.

"Which loop you thinking?" Runner asked, scratching his chin.

"We'll have to go right back to Hillston to avoid the worst of it."

The men swore.

"I know," I agreed grimly. "But with fuel and women, we're attractive targets."

"And on that cheerful note, let's get the fuck out of here." Runner slapped a hand on my shoulder. "Pope, wheel Rusty around. We'll get her filled and ready while Shield briefs the others."

"Who's on watch?" I asked.

"Texas and Butcher. Along with Switch—one of our prospects," Wrath answered, his gaze locked on the horizon. "Killer's around somewhere. She's a fucking bastard radar."

I chuckled. "Useful."

"We got another girl, too—Lottie. A vet, though she's nursing Zero rather than animals at the moment."

"Zero's here?"

"Yeah. But—" Wrath hesitated. "He's in rough shape. Real rough."

"What happened?"

"Bastard bite. Managed to save him—lost the left arm, though. He's tough but...." He shook his head.

I sobered, wincing. Bastard fluids transferred the corrupt virus from the host to a new victim. If you lived long enough to survive the initial attack, your days were numbered unless you stopped the main infection.

Removing a limb was quick, but in these days of zero hospital care, it was just as risky as the bite itself.

A good reminder of your responsibility. Don't let a pretty girl divert you from what you need to do.

I glanced around. "Where is he?"

"In the tanker's bed."

I nodded. "I'll check on him before we go. You sure you got enough fuel to spare?"

Runner's lips tipped up. "I think we can swing it."

"Then let's get her fuelled and get the fuck out of here." I tilted my head toward the growing number of people on the horizon. "Prefer not to get into another gunfight today."

"Just saying," Pope muttered as he began pushing Rusty toward the tankers. "Farmer ain't gonna be happy to see our ugly mugs once again."

My gut clenched. "You stayed with Farmer?"

Pope halted, slapping a hand to his face. "Shit. I'm a fuckwit." He nodded. "Yeah, Prez. Left there earlier today. Your sister was there. She's good. Baby is good. She's—"

My chest tightened. "Baby?"

Audrey sighed loudly, drawing my attention. "What the Neanderthal is attempting to say is that your sister, Mari, is pregnant."

I bent, feeling as if I'd been sucker punched in the gut.

A baby.

I closed my eyes, processing the chaos of emotions swamping me.

Fuck. I'm gonna be an uncle.

A million thoughts ran through my mind as I absorbed the news. So many things could go wrong. There was no health care. No midwives. This was the After. Every risk increased.

They could be lost to me.

Like Harpa.

Distantly I was aware of people disbursing, giving me space to process the shock.

A hand rested on the small of my back.

"Are you alright?" Audrey asked, her voice soft.

I straightened, nodding. "Fuck yeah."

Her gaze swept my face, her eyes big behind her glasses. "You didn't know."

"About the baby?" I shook my head.

"No," Audrey corrected. "That she was still alive."

I nodded once. "Had hoped but...."

"Nothing is guaranteed in the After," she finished for me. She pressed her hand against my back, offering me a small smile. "You can see for yourself tonight."

"Yeah."

One of the women called her name, and with a final glance, she dropped her hand and moved off, joining her friends.

It took a little time, but thankfully time was on our side.

I made my way out to where Butcher and Texas patrolled. Big and broad with tattoos and faces that said they meant business, these men had seen shit and weren't afraid to throw down when needed.

"Good to see you, Prez." Texas gestured at the tankers. "Welcome to the future."

My lips quirked. "Who'd have thought you'd be riding point to protect fuel?"

Texas chuckled. "Some *Mad Max* fuckery, for sure."

He clapped me on the back before turning to give Jo shit, shooting me an amused look when she snapped back.

I see how it is.

If Hazard hadn't taken on the job, I'd have suggested Texas for the role. Sharp as a tack and fiercely protective, he'd do what he needed to ensure our Club survived.

Butcher stood watch, his face guarded as he stared at the road ahead.

"You okay?" I asked, coming to stand beside him.

"Can't go under them. Can't go over them. Guess we gotta go through them."

My lips quirked at his use of lines from a kid's book.

He glanced at me. "We got women. We got fuel. We got ammo and food and transport. You think those fuckers are gonna let us through without a fight?"

I shook my head. "Not a chance. Good thing we're not headed that way."

Butcher raised his eyebrow. "No?"

I shook my head. "Follow me, brother. I'll show you the way."

3

SHIELD

Rusty roared under my ass, the sound of her a fucking dream after the nightmare day I'd just lived through. Scuffed and dinted, she'd held up despite the bruising the bastards had inflicted on her.

Pleased to see the road gods have my back.

I'd never again take for granted her sound, the feel of her, the wind in my face. Never had before, but especially not now. Not when I'd come so close to losing this feeling.

Freedom.

The road called to me with a siren song I was helpless to refuse.

Rusty backfired, bucking a second before settling back into a smooth ride.

The only downside to biofuel.

The crude fuel wasn't the standard I normally fed my vehicles, but beggars couldn't be choosers in the After, and I'd take what I was given and be fucking grateful for it.

Now we cruised along the dusty road, avoiding the occasional fallen tree, wild animal, or other debris as I led our motley crew away from the Purge.

Open road like this gave me time to think. The last few months, I'd been consumed with plans and pressures, weighed down by too many unsolvable problems.

Today though, all the problems fell away, leaving Audrey's voice on a loop in my head.

When? Now? Can we—?

I shook my head, trying to clear the unnatural interest this woman engendered.

It'd been a while since I'd had a woman sit on my face. It'd been even longer since I'd felt anything around my dick but some lube and my left hand. My focus had been on the Club and leading us through this painful transition. By the time shit had started to calm down, we'd been three men to one woman up at the Plantation.

As National President, I knew there were women who'd dive into bed with me, given the slightest indication of my interest. Hot, sweet, grateful women who wanted a man to feed and protect them. Some of my brothers might be happy to settle for a façade, but that had never been me. I didn't want gratitude—I wanted greedy. I wanted a woman hot and willing, who knew what she needed and wasn't afraid to ask for it.

Audrey, it seemed, was that woman.

With the approach of the Purge, I'd not had time to interrogate how Audrey and the others had joined our Club, but it was at the top of my to-do list once we stopped for the night.

To get to Cunnamulla, we'd have to double back and take a longer route through arid country, looping through hundreds of kilometres of thick red dirt and empty skies.

Gonna be a hell of a ride.

My mind ticked over, planning the inevitable.

We'll have to ration fuel and reduce the number of vehicles.

We'll need food and a fuck tonne of water. Camping supplies—creature comforts are gonna be few and far between.

Spring had hit, and summer was fast approaching. With the temperature rising, we'd need to be through the hottest parts of our trip before the zenith if we didn't want overheated vehicles and risk sun exposure.

Such was the life of those who lived in this sunburnt land.

With no other vehicles on the road, you'd have been forgiven for thinking the trip would be quick. But the roads hadn't been maintained in a few years, which meant unknown issues like dead animals, fallen trees, abandoned vehicles and potholes. The weather in this part of the country could be volatile, with floods and heat waves just par for the course. It took a strong breed to live out in the wild country—and stronger still to thrive.

I'd ridden these roads a million times visiting Chapters. Even before I'd been voted in as National President, my heart had lived for the road. Up and down the country, I'd lived for the roar of the pipes in my ears, the vibration under my ass, and the power between my thighs.

The pandemic had been a fucking nightmare come to life. Trapped in one place, dwindling fuel supplies, brothers dying, their women and family sick or dead, unable to get to Chapters across the states who needed support and guidance. I'd been wedged between a rock and a hard place, forced to make decisions that had life-and-death repercussions.

Harpa.

My bike bucked as if hearing my thought, pulling me back from the journey of self-flagellation I seemed more than willing to traverse.

You didn't know.

No amount of ration or reason would thaw the icy guilt that had frozen my chest and pierced my gut.

We crested a small hill, my brooding thoughts dispelling. Pulling onto a grated gravel and dirt road, I slowed the vehicle, guiding Rusty up a gentle incline and into the bush. The long dirt driveway wound through dense bush, the tankers bumping and protesting as the incline steepened up to the crest of a small mountain. Existing the brush into a cleared area, high fortified walls stood as a testament to the man who reigned this rural castle.

Farmer had been a buddy during our years serving overseas. When I'd gotten out, I'd fallen in with my dad's Club, finding among the membership a brotherhood and solidarity I'd sorely needed. Farmer had chosen a different path, building an elite team of private security specialists for hire, creating his own form of brotherhood.

Our experiences had marked us, leading us both down paths that had forced us to withdraw from society.

My sister, Mari, had fallen for him. And the bastard hadn't stopped her fall. He wasn't the kind of guy I'd have chosen for her. He was too rough around the edges. Too possessive.

Mari had accused me of hating him for her because he was too like me. She wasn't wrong. We were cut from the same cloth, shaped by the same experiences. I knew what went on in my mind, knew exactly what I was capable of. And if Farmer was the same, then there was no fucking way I'd let him near my sister.

At least, not in the Before. In the After, he was exactly the kind of guy she needed. Possessive. Rough around the edges. Willing to fuck the world and set it on fire to keep her safe.

No fucking way would I have chosen another man for her.

I just didn't let either of them know it.

The fortified steel gates swung open, granting us access.

When the virus had first arisen, Farmer had noped the fuck out of society early on. He'd purchased the farm and a fuck load of the land around it, stockpiled anything he could get his hands on, and stayed put.

I'd forced the Club to do the same, but some of the Chapters had been too slow or too enmeshed in the local communities to pull entirely away.

The Ipswich Chapter had been wiped clean out. Not one member—child or adult—had survived the virus.

For the better part of five years, we'd been fighting a battle we had no hope of winning. How did you keep your people safe from an enemy none of us could see?

The world hadn't gone to shit overnight. It'd disintegrated slowly, the death toll staggering its way up to a peak from which we'd never recover.

And then, as quickly as it had arrived, it disappeared, leaving the survivors to deal with a new kind of hell—the After.

I idled to a halt, eyes peeled as the trucks rumbled in behind me.

The courtyard had changed since I'd last been down this way more than a year prior. There were more animals and buildings, better fortifications and a shit ton more weaponry.

He's worried.

The hairs on the back of my neck rose, a feeling of unease stirring in my gut.

Mari.

The vehicles around me parked, the mechanical sounds

of running engines falling silent to allow in the quiet of baying sheep, calling birds and the occasional dog bark.

"You fucker."

I grinned, turning to find my brother-in-law climbing down from one of the turrets.

"Miss me?" I asked, swinging off my bike.

"Not a bit."

We met half-way, clapping each other into a back-smacking embrace.

Tall, broad, with sun-kissed skin and lightened hair, Farmer looked to be the epitome of his name. Only those who served with him knew where it had originated—and it wasn't agriculture related.

"She okay?" I asked my voice low.

"She's good," Farmer answered, giving me immediate reassurance. "You know?"

I nodded.

"Due in a few months." He shook his head, stepping back. "Scares the fuck out of me. What do I know about being a dad?"

I gestured at the activity around us. "This why you're gearing up for World War fucking Three through Sixteen?"

Farmer shook his head again. "We're seeing increases in activity in the area. People raiding, bastards hunting, militia."

"You run into any issues?"

Farmer shrugged. "Nothing we couldn't take care of."

I frowned. "Maybe we should—"

"Shield!"

Farmer and I twisted, both of us grinning as Mari waddled across the courtyard.

"Jesus," I muttered as Farmer and I headed for my sister. "How far along is she?"

"Fuck if I know. She says five months, but...." He gestured at Mari.

Shorter than me by at least half, she took after our grandmother in stature and looks. Brunette hair and tan skin paired with striking blue eyes. She came no higher than the middle of my chest, her petite build failing to hide her burgeoning belly.

There was no way in hell my sister was only five months along.

I met her mid-way across the foreyard, scooping her up to wrap her in a tight hug. Her belly pressed into me, my grip awkward but firm. Mari was as familiar to me as my own heart, and yet these changes in her were different and unexpected—throwing me into a dance with unexpected grief.

Our lives progressed even when we were separated. Despite my desire to wrangle time into a pause, it charged forth, one-second tumbling after another.

Shoving my melancholy thoughts away, I breathed deeply, I relished her sweet, familiar smell.

"Hey, baby sis," I whispered, holding her tight.

At my greeting, Mari's control broke, her hands turning into claws that gripped my kutte, her voice breaking as she sobbed out a welcome.

"I h-h-hate you!"

I chuckled into her hair. "I love you too, Mari."

She pulled back a fraction, staring up at me with glistening eyes. "You came."

"I said I would."

"You're late."

I chuckled, gently setting her back on the group. "I know. Forgive me?"

She reached up to cup my cheeks in her palms, searching my face. "I worried."

I closed my eyes, letting her words sink in. "The Plantation got hit. The virus was followed by waves of bastards and then militia. They needed me."

She nodded once. "I understand."

I wrapped her back in a hug. "I'm sorry, Mari. I promised and failed."

The last time I'd left here had been just before the world went dark. Just before all the communications were killed off by the government and whole cities were blown to bits.

"Have you heard from her?" she asked, her voice soft.

I hesitated, knowing I was about to break her heart. "No, I'm sorry."

Mari drew in a shuddering breath, then stepped back, catching one of my hands to rest it on her belly. "If it's a girl, we'll call her Harpa."

The breath punched out of my chest.

Harpa.

Guilt, anger, frustration, grief, hope—these were the emotions boiling under my surface, singing through my veins, forcing me to confront reality.

I cleared my throat. "She'll love that."

Tears welled in Mari's eyes, shimmering on her lashes. "You think she's still alive."

It was a statement, not a question.

"She's a fighter. She's resourceful. She'll do what she has to." I leaned forward to press my forehead against hers. "I believe she's alive, Mari. I have to."

Mari pressed our hands closer to her skin. "I think so too."

As if hearing us, there was movement under my palm.

"Is that—?"

Mari nodded, a tear falling down her cheek.

Fuck, but it wrecked me to see it. There was nothing I wanted more for my sister than a happy life, but the virus had ripped that away. Now everything was tinged with bittersweet regrets, joy and grief cohabitating the same spaces.

I glanced up to find Audrey watching us, an expression I couldn't quite read written on her face. Before I could consider her further, Mari drew my attention back to her.

"Would you like something to eat?" she asked, swiping away the last of her tears. "And perhaps a shower?"

I laughed, slinging one arm around her shoulders and allowing her to guide me across the foreyard.

"Sounds perfect."

4

AUDREY

In my life, I had experienced many types of leaders. There were some like my parents, who were authoritative and briskly disciplinary. They wielded their power as if they deserved it, demanding respect without actually taking the time to cultivate it.

There were those where the mantle of leadership had been thrust upon them. These were people who led because they'd reached a sufficient level of seniority or because the hierarchy of their position demanded such managerial oversight. Some of these people were good at what they did, they learnt on the job and made an effort to ensure that the people under them were supported. But for those in this group, their newfound requirement sat uncomfortably. They were like the medieval Christians who wore itchy hair shirts as punishments to atone for their sins—and so their new management was a punishment for their promotion.

And then there was the third type of person, the true leaders. This group was far rarer and more precious than any I had known. These were the people who were not created leaders, they were born to it. They carried a cloak of power around them, their presence calming and comforting. They were neither flashy nor abrasive. They were who you looked to instinctively. They were who you'd seek out in an emergency. They were who you trusted to know what to do.

Shield struck me as one such man.

Upon our meeting, I'd noted the respect paid to him by the members of his Club. They treated him with deference and affection—or as much as a biker showed. They listened to him attentively, each walking away from their interaction with seemingly lighter loads.

He'd led us away from the Purge with little haste or concern, his patience and calm an attractive contrast to the chaotic world in which no we found ourselves.

As we'd followed him down the winding paths back to the Farm, I'd wondered if this respect and interest would extend to the women in our group.

Now I had my answer.

Hiding behind a large post in the barn, I covertly watched as Shield conversed with Jo, both of them bent to examine his motorcycle.

The barn's comforting smell of hay, old leather, and musty wood mixed with the sharp bite of oil and gasoline, the mix strangely pleasant. It reminded me of long afternoons spent reading under my grandfather's workbench as he pottered around the garden shed, muttering swear words to himself in Vietnamese, assuming I would never understand.

I shoved the memory away, locking that Pandora's box of emotion.

For the last few hours, I'd stalked Shield as he'd made his way around the farm, connecting with his sister and others he knew and introducing himself to the women in our party.

I liked that. A lot.

It also didn't hurt that he looked like the kind of man who could take care of business. Average height but broad with a mop of dark brown hair peppered with salt at his temples. I put him at mid-to-late thirties, maybe even early forties, his face a testament to a life full of laughter.

He gestured at his bike, making a shape with his hands and calling my attention to them. He had big hands, strong with the kind of blunt fingers that I wanted to feel running over my body.

How long has it been? Three years? Four? Too long.

"What are you doing?"

I startled, whipping around to find Pope leaning against the side of the building, arms crossed, watching me with a small smirk.

In the Before, one might have mistaken Pope for a movie star or bad boy rocker. Far too pretty for his own good, I had no doubt that his bed had rarely been empty even after the virus had decimated the female population.

"Observing Shield," I answered easily. "I'm collating data."

He chuckled, shaking his head. "Audrey, don't ever change."

I tilted my head to one side. "Why would you wish stagnation upon someone? Change is how we learn and evolve. It's through evolution that our species learned to not only survive but thrive. Change is how you and I are still here, living while the billions of others who refused to adapt died."

His smile widened. "I stand corrected. Always change."

I nodded once. "I will."

He pushed off the wall coming to stand beside me and peer around the pole. "So why are you spying on the Prez?"

I bristled. "I'm not spying. I'm *assessing*."

"And what are you assessing then?"

"His character. I'm considering inviting him to have sex with me. "

Pope stiffened, jerking upright and turning around to stare at me. "So, you'll sleep with him but not me?"

It was my turn to chuckle. "You're not interested in me." I reached out to pat his shoulder. "You're funny."

"No?" He lifted his arm to run his knuckles lightly down my cheek. "You sure about that?"

I pulled back, rolling my eyes. "Yes. If you'd wanted that from me, you'd have offered it weeks ago. I've seen your modus operandi. You enjoy quantity over quality."

"What can I say?" he asked, spreading his arms wide. "I'm a purveyor of pleasure."

"Besides," I continued, ignoring his interruption. "I intimidate you. You find it hard to be sexually attracted to anyone you respect."

His lips quirked into a wry grin. "Anyone ever told you you're too smart for your own good?"

A memory rose sharp and jarring.

You're too smart for your own good. No one will want you.

I shook off the shiver of unease that slithered down my spine.

Not today, Satan.

"Eighteen people, three of whom were related to me." I twisted away from Pope to peek back around the solid beam. The thick ancient wood lay cool and smooth under my palm, the roughened edges polished from years of friction. Wider than two of me standing side by side, the wood pole stretched up the full three stories to the roof of the ancient but functional barn.

Almost absently, my mind opened a box labelled trees, beginning to cycle through the years of useless facts I'd collected.

Gum trees can grow to—

My thoughts stuttered to silence as Shield dropped into a crouch beside his bike, his head bent as he listened to Jo point something out on the rear of the motorcycle.

Oh my.

His ass deserved its own shrine. On some level I knew I was objectifying him. On every other level, I didn't care.

It'd been a long time since a man had entered my bed. Longer still since I'd allowed one to enter me.

Pope sighed heavily, drawing my attention from Shield's perfect ass. "You want him."

His statement didn't surprise me. If nothing else, Pope could be relied upon for honesty.

Well, with me at least.

"I might," I admitted, not wanting to fully reveal what I was thinking.

Hint. It began and ended with hubba.

"He's solid, Audrey. Trust me."

Despite being our resident whore of Babylon, Pope was a good guy. If I'd ever had an older brother, he would have been the kind of older brother I hoped I'd have had. Easy to talk to, funny, accepting. He respected me and treated me as an equal—and I appreciated that more than I could ever articulate.

"I do," I told him truthfully. "But I want to gauge my level of interest before I decide if he's worthy of seduction."

Pope's eyes sparkled with amusement.

"Seduction, huh? And what does that look like?"

And there was the downside to having him in an older brother role—he could be annoying as a mosquito in a bedroom right before you're falling asleep.

I shot him an annoyed look. "I know you're making fun of me."

He pressed a hand to his chest, acting wounded. "Me? Never!"

I turn my back on him.

"You still gonna play me in poker tonight?" he asked, slinging an arm around my shoulders.

"No."

"Why not?"

I watched Shield laugh at something Jo said. His amusement pulled a begrudging smile from my stoic friend, her lips curling up ever so slightly.

"You're a sore loser," I answered, trying to ignore the little tingle of jealousy that had taken root as I watched Shield and Jo.

"You wound me."

I glanced up at Pope. "You accused me of cheating."

"You counted cards."

I rolled my eyes. "I didn't. I just made statistically accurate predictions."

And discovered your tell after two rounds.

Though that knowledge would go with me to my grave.

"Bullshit, you—" his gaze slipped away from mine, his grin easy. "Hey, Prez."

I stiffened, becoming hyperaware of a presence behind me.

"Pope, Audrey," Shield's greeting sent pleasant shivers twinkling down my spine. "You two alright?"

His voice sounded distant; his tone cool.

I didn't like it. It wasn't at all similar to the warm

humour he'd displayed upon our first meeting or the easy companionship he'd offered Jo.

A niggle of uncertainty took root in my belly, a combination of jealousy and confusion.

Determined to recapture that easy chemistry, I twisted out from under Pope's arm and stepped closer to Shield. He crossed his arms, planting his feet as his gaze swung from Pope to me and back.

"We are living through a society-ending event," I told Shield, my mouth running faster than my brain could process. "I have been forced to reconcile killing people in the name of my own survival. The first few times were difficult, but bastards, I'm learning, are easier to kill than militia or Purge. I suspect that reflects my personal belief that the humanity within them would wish me to end their suffering and reduce their impact on those of us that remain."

For a beat, neither Pope nor Shield spoke.

"So, in answer to your question," I concluded. "I am satisfactory."

Shield's arms loosened, the stiffness in his shoulders easing as his expression warmed, a twinkle lightening his expression.

"I'm glad." He shot a glance at Pope. "You need me?"

Pope shook his head, tucking his hands into his pockets. "Nope. Just checking in to let you know that dinner will be ready in thirty." He grinned, spinning on his heel. "I'll see you guys in the mess hall."

I watched Shield watch Pope walking away.

"We're not together," I told him, determined to kill any doubts in his mind. "Nor have we ever been, in case that's a turn-off for you."

Shield's eyebrows rose. "A turn-off?"

I nodded. "You might be one of those men who refuse to

sleep with women their friends have been with. Don't worry, I haven't slept with anyone in your Club."

"Ah, good to know."

I nodded again, pleased he understood. "I would have liked to, but the truth is none of them are quite right."

Shield leaned against the pole beside him, arms crossed, one leg crossing over the other. "No?"

"I'm sure they're perfectly lovely individuals, but I am looking for something specific."

The corner of Shield's mouth tipped up. "And what would that be?"

"A man who isn't expecting commitment."

He cocked an eyebrow. "And you think that's me?"

I nodded earnestly. "You're perfect."

"Am I? Do tell."

I lifted my hand, ticking off his attributes on my fingers.

"You're bossy—I can already tell. You know what you want and appear to be both easily amused and amusing. You're large with attractive hands."

He held his hands out in front of him, staring at their backs with a mock frown. "I've never noticed their beauty before."

"That's because they belong to you. No one notices what is most beautiful about them unless they're a narcissist, actively looking, or having embraced years of body-positive therapy."

He dropped his hands. "Tell me how else I'm perfect."

I was more than happy to oblige. "You have responsibilities and duties, which means you won't be interested in long-term arrangements."

"Says who?"

I stumbled over my words, surprised by his statement. "You want a commitment?"

He lifted one arm in a half-shrug. "The world can be a lonely place."

I frowned. "That's not in the cards for us."

"No? You sure about that?"

I lifted my chin. "Positive."

"Because you're young and gorgeous, and I'm old and washed up—granted, with attractive hands?"

His teasing didn't soothe the unease his question had raised.

"Because relationships lead to death."

Shield frowned. "That's harsh."

I shrugged. "That's reality."

He shifted closer, his gaze transmitting compassion and understanding. "Someone hurt you."

Stop.

"No," I brushed away his concern before it could manifest into sympathy. "I'm just a realist. Relationships are complications. When you care for people, it's harder to survive."

"Explain."

I shuffled from foot to foot, trying to find the words to describe what I meant.

"When the world began to end, family units bunkered down. They cared for their loved ones, determined to stay with them until the end. They wanted to say goodbye and grieve over a carcass that no longer held the spirit of their deceased. That dedication is what killed them. It's what assisted the rapid transmission of the disease."

Shield let out a low whistle. "That's some dark shit you're harbouring."

I shrugged. "Data doesn't lie."

"Maybe."

I bristled at his dismissive tone. "Are you saying data lies?"

"It can be manipulated."

I waved a hand. "That is human intervention."

His lips quirked. "Are you saying you're not human, darlin'?"

"No, I'm saying I don't manipulate data."

He smirked. "Never?"

The lie fell easily from my lips. "Never."

He made a humming sound under his breath. "Come on." He turned on his heel, beginning to stroll away from me.

"Where?" I asked, following him like a stray puppy.

"You'll see."

He led me passed Jo, who raised her eyebrows but said nothing as she tinkered with his bike.

Out into the fading sunlight, Shield captured my hand, guiding me through the bustling, dusty forecourt and across to one of the main buildings.

As we walked in silence, I began to catalogue the differences in our touch, our sizes, the way we walked and moved. He strode across the forecourt, his large, calloused touch possessive and bold. I suspected he didn't realise or, perhaps, he didn't care what his actions conveyed.

Sex, Audrey. This is just about sweaty, filthy, yummy sex. Remember?

Frustration simmered under my skin. The thoughts in my head were louder than they had been in years.

In the Before, I had options to quiet them—medication, gym sessions, sex, therapy. In the After, the thoughts had become intrusive and no matter how hard I pushed myself, no matter how exhausted I made my body, the fear fed the noise. Panic and fear left me awake in the middle of the night, spinning scenario after scenario, crunching numbers and contemplating every decision that led us to now.

I need a sweaty sex session and the delicious endorphins that will bring. That's all I need. Endorphins.

Shield led me around the corner of an outbuilding, and I stumbled, blinking when I realised where he was taking me.

"You want me to help in the kitchen?" I asked as he led me to a door marked with a whisk.

"Nope." He shoved it open and pulled me in. "I want you to take a seat while I cook."

I frowned. "Why?"

"Why what?" he asked, reaching for a waist apron and tying it on.

"Wouldn't I be more use helping?"

He grinned. "Don't worry, you'll be of use. But I need your brain, not your hands... at least not yet."

Pacified, I took a seat at the counter, watching as he began to bustle around the room, seemingly familiar with the layout.

"I lived here for a month or so after Mari and Farmer shacked up," he explained, answering my unspoken question.

I propped my elbows on the counter to rest my chin on my hands. "What are you making?"

"A cake."

"For Mari?"

He nodded. "She deserves to celebrate."

A warm glittery feeling shimmered down my spine. "That's nice of you."

"That's love."

My nose wrinkled. "You disagree with my stance on relationships."

"A hundred percent," he said cheerfully, holding no heat. "But I think I understand."

I watched him move for a beat longer, strangely lulled by his confident, deliberate movements. His biceps flexed, drawing attention to his wealth of muscles.

Without meaning to, I began to categorise where he fell within the 'attractive biceps of men I know' list.

He has better definition than Runner and more bulk than Pope. But he doesn't have tattoos like Butcher or cross his arms anywhere near as much as Ghost. In a comparison to Texas, I'd put him at a solid—

"Tell me about your network."

I blinked, drawn from my thoughts by his unexpected question.

"What do you want to know?"

"Does it work?"

I scoffed. "Of course, it works."

"How?"

"Same way mobiles worked in the Before."

He paused in his measuring of flour. "But the government jammed the signals. They destroyed everything. Even fucking two-way doesn't work for further than a kilometre. We had Morse code for a while, but even that got blasted."

I shrugged. "Sure, none of that works now. But I don't need it. A-Frequency is a different beast."

I watched his lips quirk, once again struck by how easily he smiled.

"A-Frequency?"

"My network, my name."

He chuckled, tossing the flour into a bowl and reaching for eggs. "I like it. So, you essentially by-passed known frequencies?"

"If you'd like to simplify what I did, then yes." I leaned

forward, watching him skilfully crack the eggs without dropping shells into the mix.

How does he do that?

One could safely say the culinary arts were not my forte. People had said it was like science—all measurements and precision. Well, I'd never had to eat my science experiments.

"Why do you ask?" I asked, pulling myself back from my thoughts.

"We need eyes and ears. The bastards are on the move, people are getting desperate. The viral danger may have passed, but the real issue is what comes next." He lifted a whisk and stuck it into the sticky mix, briskly whipping it around the bowl. "Make no mistakes, Audrey. It's gonna get a fucking shit ton worse before it gets better."

The hairs on the back of my neck rose as my mind began to conjure up millions of scenarios. Based on current resources, available weaponry, and my best guesses about food sources, three scenarios stood out.

"You think we're going to have wars."

He nodded grimly. "I've been travelling for weeks. There are roadblocks everywhere. Towns overtaken by tyrants. Militia sweeping through areas searching for women, fighting for food, shitting on anyone who might stand in their way. Those looking for peace aren't gonna find it."

I shivered. "Why do you need me?"

"Runner says your brain is like a computer." He paused in his stirring to lift the whisk and test the batter's consistency. "I need you to crunch options."

"Options like...?"

"Like keeping the three chapters separate or consolidating them. Like working out the risks associated with moving that many people, animals and equipment. Like the risks of not diversifying our production options. Like how the fuck I keep my people safe in a world that seems determined to destroy them."

I couldn't hide my disappointment, the taste sharp and bitter on my tongue.

Shield needed my brain. Like every other person in the world, he wanted what I could do, not who I was.

Did you expect anything different?

I knit my fingers together, dropping my hands into my lap as I stared down at them.

"When do you need the analysis?"

I sounded normal if distant, the cold that had kept me safe began to wrap its icy chill back around my heart.

You're good at this, Audrey. This is why they keep you around. Goodness knows it's the only thing you're good at.

"As soon as you can."

"I'll get started tonight." I lifted my head, straightening my shoulders. "I'll need more information. I'll need everything you can share on the chapters. On their needs, the people, the spaces. Food stores, locations, skills. Personalities. The more you can tell me, the better the analysis."

Shield nodded, turning his attention back to the mixing bowl. "Thank you."

I slid off the stool, readying to leave. "Is that all?"

"No."

I braced, awaiting his next request.

"I want to hear more about you sitting on my face."

5

AUDREY

I blinked at Shield's unexpected comment.

Did he really just...?

I shoved my glasses up my nose, leaning across the counter. "I sometimes have trouble telling the difference between sincerity and sarcasm. Are you being sincere?"

"Absolutely." He reached for a jar of something dark and sticky. I expected him to drop his gaze and refocus on what he was doing, but his hands moved while his eyes remained locked on mine. "Were you?"

"I'm always sincere," I said, returning to my seat as I watched him tilt the jar over the cake batter. "The problem is other people. They mask what they should just say. They say I'm too blunt or honest. But how can that be when all I say is the truth?"

A slow drizzle of syrup fell from the jar to pool in the middle of the batter. The scent of it rich and sweet.

My mouth watered with the need to taste.

"I like honesty." Shield's tone put me in mind of the syrup—warm and rich. "Even in a Club as well adjusted as this one, there's bullshit. I trust my brothers but sometimes they'll say one thing when their actions indicate another intention."

A scenario began to unfold in my head—one involving Shield spreading me over the kitchen counter and making good use of that jar.

I nodded, trying to ignore the scenario spinning in my head. "People are duplicitous. When working out scenarios, they are always the factor that creates the wildest variations. You have one person who undermines the plan, and it all goes sour."

Shield caught the end of the syrup trail with his finger as he tilted the jar up. "I agree."

I watched him set down the jar on the bench and reach for a rag.

"Wait." I leaned across the bench to wrap my fingers around his wrist. "Can I taste?"

His eyebrows lifted, a grin pulling up one side of his handsome face. "Be my guest."

He held his finger up to my lips. I flicked my tongue out to give the sticky sweet syrup a testing lick.

Honey.

Enjoying the flavour bursting across my tongue, I let out a little moan of pleasure.

I silently labelled this scenario 69—best case, Shield decided he wanted to taste me while his cake baked. Worst case, he'd let me down gently.

Nothing ventured, nothing gained.

"I miss sweets," I muttered before flicking my tongue out again to scoop more of the honey from his skin. "So much."

Shield cleared his throat but didn't respond. I glanced up to find his gaze locked on my mouth, a muscle jumping in his jaw.

Jaw tight, pulse elevated, breathing irregular, face flushed.

My heart fell, visions of scenario 69 evaporating.

"Are you angry?" I asked, tilting my head to one side. "Did you want to lick it up instead?"

"No," he ground out, his voice rough and low. "I want to lick *you*."

Arousal unfurled in my belly, my hopes rising.

"Where?"

"Everywhere."

I grinned. "When?"

"Now."

I pointed at his batter. "Perhaps you should finish your cake first?"

"Fuck the cake."

I crossed my arms over my chest. "But it's for your sister and her unborn baby."

Shield's jaw clenched, and I made a mental note that he looked angry when he was aroused.

I like it.

"Fine," he bit out. "Cake first, then dessert."

"Am I dessert?" I asked, delighted by the idea.

He snatched up his whisk, aggressively whipping the batter. "Yes."

I hopped down from my chair and took a step back. "We're all staying in the barn. We'll need to find somewhere quiet where people won't interrupt us. I don't like to be interrupted."

"I know a place."

I nodded. "And we'll need to shower first."

His arm stilled. "Okay...."

"And you'll need to brush your teeth."

"I didn't realise my breath was bad."

"It's not. But we can't risk thrush. Not when we have little medicine to spare."

His lips curled into a smile. "I see. Anything else?"

I frowned, tapping the side of my cheek with a finger. "We'll need to discuss boundaries. I assume you have a condom?"

He nodded.

"And safe words. Also, what will happen after."

"After?"

I nodded. "After I sleep with you. I may want seconds. I may not."

He dropped the bowl onto the bench and rounded the counter. Snagging me by my waist, Shield hauled me into his chest, one hand securing me to him, the other delving into my hair to hold my head in place.

"You'll want seconds," he promised. As if to prove it, his mouth captured mine in a hungry kiss. If I were honest, kiss was too benign a word for what he did. Fuck perhaps described it better. He fucked my mouth, demanding I open for him and marking territory that would soon be his.

I felt branded by him. Overwhelmed. Aroused and needing. My blood pounded in my ears and pooled in my abdomen. Wet heat slicked my labia, an empty ache settling in my middle.

Touch me.

Shield slowed our kiss in increments, banking but not extinguishing the roaring need he'd stoked between us.

"Maybe," I murmured when he finally lifted his head. "You should fuck the cake."

His chuckle sent warm air brushing my cheek. "Let me get this in the oven and tell someone to keep an eye on it. I'll meet you at the shower block."

I sighed, tilting my head back to meet his gaze. "You didn't bump my glasses."

He grinned. "Not my first rodeo." He pressed a kiss to my nose then let me go.

Without his arms around me, I felt strangely bereft. Like a ship lost at sea, bopping around without any sense of direction.

What a horrid thought. You do not need a man to guide you when you are your own moon and stars.

I stepped back, putting space between us.

"I look forward to our cunnilingus session," I told him, nodding briskly.

His chuckle followed me from the room. "As do I."

6

———

AUDREY

I slipped into the shower block and found Jo scrubbing her hands at one of the basins, dressed in a too-large and stained overalls that drowned her.

The Besser block building put me in mind of dreaded school camps from years long gone. Cracked concrete, cheap tiles, and exposed metal piping coupled with dim lighting to add to the murder vibe.

"Yo," Jo said, giving me a head tilt as she scrubbed her hands in the chipped porcelain basin. "You looking for me?"

I shook my head. "No, I'm going for a shower." I couldn't keep the glee from my tone. "Shield agreed to perform cunnilingus on me."

Jo's eyes narrowed. "Oh, he did, did he?" She flicked the water from her hands before turning off the facet. "And what else did he agree to exactly?"

"Nothing at the moment, but I'm hopeful he may agree to penetration."

Jo's eyes drifted closed as she lifted one hand to pinch the bridge of her nose. "Forgive me Father for my past sins. I see my penance has arrived." Sucking in a deep breath, she dropped her hands and pegged me with a look. "Audrey, you do know that you don't have to sleep with him."

I nodded, dancing from side to side. "But I want to. Have you seen his hands?"

Her lips quirked, then thinned into a serious line. "I know you're keen to get your rocks off—"

"Climax," I corrected her. "I'm hopeful he may be the person to push me to orgasm."

"Tomato, tom-ah-to," she said, fluttering her hands around. "Point is, I know you've been holding out for a while. I mean, fuck, none of these men are exactly subtle. So why him? Why now?"

I lifted one shoulder in a half-shrug. "His pheromones call to me. This is purely primal."

She hesitated. "Audrey, he's not some escort you can just fuck and leave. He doesn't strike me as a fuck buddy, either. He's got roots in this Club. He's got ties that go deeper than blood or family. His loyalty is to them. You sure you want to be fucking a man who would throw you to the wolves if you were a risk to his Club?"

Absolutely.

"I know what I'm getting into," I promised. "He knows this is casual. One and done. Or maybe two, and we're through. Three, and you gotta leave me, if I really like it. Or perhaps—"

Jo held up a hand. "I get it. But my point stands. This guy isn't your run-of-the-mill MC member. He's the big-wig president. He's used to having people follow his orders and get his way. You sure you want that in your bed?"

I shivered in anticipation. "Oh, I do. I absolutely do." I tilted my head to one side. "Do you not?"

She snorted. "Fuck no. I've had enough guys in my life

telling me what to do. I don't need another one ordering me around. If I wanted that, I'd go back to the fucking farm."

The 'fucking farm' had been the commune Jo and her sisters, Beth and Ruby, had grown up on. There they'd been considered nothing but breeding stock, their only choices in life were to become spinsters for God or a mother of a hundred babies.

Jo had left, and when her sisters were old enough, she'd pulled them out of that life as well.

"What do you like then?" I asked, genuinely curious.

"Audrey." She pinched the bridge of her nose. "I don't want to get into this with you."

I eyed her. "Are you a virgin?"

"What?" she yelped, a flush creeping up her neck.

"Oh, you are." I laughed, delighted by the discovery. "It's okay. You can admit it."

"Audrey, please, for the love of—"

"You're a virgin?"

Jo and I turned to see Butcher and Texas standing in the doorway, their gazes locked on Jo. Big, broad and tanned from time spent under the sun, they had a plethora of tattoos and a look about them that said, 'I will fuck you up'.

"No!" Jo denied her face now scarlet. "Audrey's pontificating. She doesn't know what she—"

"Happy to take care of that for you," Texas offered, his grin that of a cat who'd eaten the canary. "You don't have to do anything. Just lay back and enjoy."

"Fuck you." Jo snatched a bar of soap from the sink and pegged it at his face. Texas easily slapped it aside with a laugh as she stormed her way past them and outside.

"Did I say something wrong?" I asked.

"Not at all," Texas drawled, turning to watch Jo stomp

her way across the yard. "You've just given me an insight I wouldn't have otherwise had."

Pleased I'd helped, I eyed them both. "Why are you here?"

Butcher raised his own eyebrow. "To bath?"

"Could you take a seat, please?" I requested, pointing at the chairs lining one wall. "Shield is coming, and I need us to be prioritised."

Butcher's lips twitched. "Would that be because you want to do the hanky panky with him?"

I nodded. "We have agreed to cunnilingus to start. Do you happen to know if he is circumcised?"

"And that's my cue to leave." He turned on his heel, fisting Texas' kutte dragging him along as he strode for the door. "Have fun, Audrey."

"I will."

Watching them scatter like cockroaches in the night, I couldn't help but wonder what I'd said.

7

AUDREY

I turned on the tap to the shower as someone rapped knuckles against the closed stall door.

"I'm in here," I called, holding a hand under the water to test the temperature.

"That's what I'm hoping."

I shivered, pleasant goosebumps prickling across my skin. "I'm just about to shower. I'll be out in a moment."

"How about I join you?"

I froze, staring at the water running over my hand. "J-join me?"

"Is that a no?"

I spun, unlocked the door and threw it open, pleased to see Shield's gaze immediately drop to my naked body.

"Not at all," I answered happily. "Please, come in."

Shield stepped through and kicked the door shut, reaching behind him to twist the lock. Steam from the shower began to coil through the space, the moist heat deliciously erotic against my skin.

This was such a good idea.

"You seem to be missing a few clothes," he murmured, his gaze sliding down my body.

I glanced down, wondering if he saw the same things I did. Sun had turned my skin into a rich golden beige, the tan lines now less stark and more integrated in gradients echoing out from my torso. My ebony hair brushed my shoulders and collarbone, while a dark thatch covered my pubis.

I'd long ago given up shaving my legs and underarms, deciding such a frivolous beauty activity made no sense in the After. For one, razors were hard to come by. For another, hot water and decent soap had to be savoured.

Stretch marks touched areas on my thighs and hips, the white marks pale and unique. Like the stripes on a zebra or the marks on a giraffe, each represented an experience unique to me and my body.

Shield stepped closer, crowding me against the stall wall. He braced one hand above my head as he leaned in, the other grazed my hip, his fingers slowly travelling up my side.

I sighed, my eyelids drifting to half-mast as I observed him. His size could have overwhelmed me, but instead, I felt small and protected, ready for him to cuddle or fuck me—whatever he wished.

"You wanna be a good girl for me?" Shield asked, his voice low and rough.

The perfectionist people pleaser in me rose in answer to his question.

"Yes."

I shivered, enjoying the glint of hunger in his gaze.

"Undress me."

Eager to please, I reached for his kutte, sliding the dusty, worn leather from his body. I moved to drop it on the floor but he caught my fist with his hand, holding me in place.

"No, darlin'. We hang the kutte up. You aren't in the Club just yet, but I'll give you a quick intro. You always treat a brother's colours with respect. Kutte's represent your position in the Club. They represent your connection, the brotherhood, family. They represent the freedom, Audrey. They represent a choice we've made to become more than about ourselves." He let go of my hand. "Hang it with care."

The leather felt heavy in my hand as I reached over to hang it on a hook on the back of the door.

I wasn't sure how to feel about his statement about me not being in the Club. I'd assumed I was based solely on their acceptance of us. I also wasn't sure how to feel about the implication that the Club was a brotherhood—a patriarchal ideal that felt dated and exclusionary.

Why do you care if you don't wish to belong?

Shrugging off my uneasy, I turned back to the man in front of me, sighing a little as my glasses began to fog in the heat.

"Do you need them?" Shield asked, his hands gliding up my neck to cup my ears, his fingers touching the ends of my glasses frame.

"Only if I want to see."

He chuckled. "How much can you see if I take these off?"

"Depends on how close you are."

He stepped closer. "How's this?"

A pleasant shiver raced down my spine. "I can live with this."

Gently he removed my glasses, folding the arms and placing the spectacles on a small shelf next to my folded clothes and towel.

"This okay?" He asked, returning to cup my face with one big hand.

"Yes, I can see you."

"Good. Now keep undressing me."

My fingers fumbled with the bottom of his shirt, the material worn soft from use. Hauling it up his body, I couldn't stop my satisfied sigh as inch after inch of delicious skin was revealed.

Husky. That's what he was. Husky, muscular, bulk. The kind of body that would have been described as a 'DadBod' in the Before.

Well, call me Mummy 'cause I wanted to crawl all over him.

"Like what you see?" he asked, his lips twitching as I tossed his shirt onto the shelf behind me.

"Mm," I hummed. "You don't shave."

Thick, coarse hairs tumbled across my palms as I ran my hands over his chest.

His grin packed a bunch. "I'm not one of your prep school boys, Audrey. Waxing might be something Pope would do, but that isn't me." He dropped his head, sliding his nose along mine until our lips were a fraction apart.

"But don't worry," he whispered. "I'll take care of you."

His lips captured mine in a demanding kiss. No—there was no demand here, only possession. Shield took what he wanted, caressing open my lips to taste the inside of my mouth.

Despite his hunger, he appeared in no rush to devour, taking his time to savour our kiss, drawing it out until one kiss became both another and another.

It's like an infinity loop, at once individual and together.

I fumbled with his belt buckle, desperate to get us naked and clean.

If he's this good at kissing, he'll know how to make me come.

Succeeding in my efforts, I shoved the jeans down his hips, taking his underwear with me.

Shield chuckled, withdrawing from our kiss as I whimpered a protest.

He chuckled as he toed off his boots and, ripped off his socks, then removed his remaining clothes.

Dressed only in the dim light of the shower blocks, I drank my fill.

"You remind me of an avenging warrior—all big and broad and fierce." My gaze dropped to his penis, noting he was uncircumcised. "And erect."

He chuckled, reaching down to fist his cock. "Thank you." He gave himself one hard fist. "Get in the shower, Audrey."

I turned, stumbling a little in my haste to comply. Stepping under the warm water, I tipped my head back, enjoying the sensation of heat as it cascaded over my body.

Shield cupped my breasts from behind, his chest pressing against my back, his erection hard against my ass as he gently palmed my breasts.

"Hand me the soap."

Complying, I melted against him as he began to run the bar over my chest, up across my shoulders, down my arms and back.

"Not going to eat you out until tonight," he murmured, nuzzling my ear. "But I'll take care of you. Don't you worry."

Shield washed me, then set me aside slightly to run the soap over his own body in brisk, utilitarian motions before stepping under the spray to rinse off.

Leaning against the tiled wall of the shower, I couldn't help but reach down, trailing my fingers down my torso, over my abdomen to tangle in my curls.

"No."

His barked order stopped my movement. "No?"

He wrapped his hand around my wrist, drawing my hand away.

"Tonight, I touch you."

His hands trailed up my inner thighs, finding my pussy. Gently, he tangled fingers in my curls, parting my lips. With gentle, teasing touches, Shield began to taunt me, his gaze locked on mine as he drew panting gasps.

"Oh," I sighed, pressing my hips forward in a silent entreaty. "That feels incredible."

"Lips, Audrey."

I tilted my head back, offering him my mouth and was not at all surprised when he took it. The water shut off, the silence filled by my greedy whimpers and his murmured approval.

Sensations flowed until I couldn't distinguish one from another, until I was balanced on a precipice, willing to dive over. His mouth was ravenous, stroking, sucking, licking—our tongues clashing as he worked my body, pushing me harder and harder.

More. More. More. More.

A stray thought entered my mind, unbidden and unwanted—and distracting as hell.

If the Bastards arrived now, I'm not sure I'd hear them.

It took the edge off, and I wanted to scream with frustration as my potential orgasm began to slip away.

I'd definitely hear the militia, though. There are too many of them, and they don't give a fuck about being quiet. The ones we should be worried about are the individuals. Farmer could take one in without knowing what they're capable of. They could murder us in our sleep.

The chances of that happening must be—

Shit. It's high. Farmer needs to know. I need to tell him right now before—

I sighed heavily, reaching down to grip Shield's hand and halt him.

Really, Audrey? You couldn't have faked it?

I never faked anything, and it wasn't fair to allow him to continue when there was no chance of an orgasm now that I was in a scenario cycle.

It was nice while it lasted.

Men, I'd found, rarely asked for a second go when you stopped them mid-coitus attempt. They tended to take it as a personal affront to their ego.

Shield grunted, withdrawing a fraction. "What's wrong?"

I shook my head. "It's no use. I'm not going to come this afternoon."

He blinked. "Why the fuck not?"

I tapped the side of my head. "I need to go work out a scenario. It's important."

"And you thought of that now? Just now?"

I nodded sadly. "It's a curse."

He eyed me, and I was pleased to note that his lips were red and slightly swollen. "You're serious."

I rocked back and forth on my heels, my fingers itching for a pen. "Yes."

He frowned, removing his hand from between my legs. "This happen often?"

I shrugged. "Often enough."

Try every time.

Shield's gaze searched my face. 'You're not happy."

"No. I wanted an orgasm."

He stepped back, allowing me to move to where my towel sat. I began to dry off as he watched me.

"Audrey?"

I glanced his way, aware of the embarrassed flush to my cheeks.

He looked like a glowering warrior, his arms crossed over his chest, his cock erect and jutting.

"Promise you'll let me try again after dinner?"

I blinked. "Wait. You *want* to try again?"

His lips quirked. "Fuck yes."

I hesitated, then shrugged. "Sure. But I can't guarantee I won't do this again."

He chuckled. "Trust me, and we'll make sure it doesn't."

I didn't believe him, but I was willing to let him try.

8

———

AUDREY

Over dinner, Shield presented his planned route, explaining it would take us through the Sturt National Park and down through backroads and around remote areas in order to get to Cunnamulla.

"We have a problem." I tapped my finger on the map. "I don't have enough transmitters for your new route."

Our small group—minus Zero—were crowded around a battered wooden table. Half-eaten bowls of kangaroo stew with freshly baked bread dotted spaces that weren't dominated by the old, worn map Shield had smoothed out.

"How short are we?" Runner asked from across the table, one arm curled around Ellie's shoulders.

I did some rapid calculations, pursing my lips. "At least three. And that's if I push everything between here and Cunnamulla to the edge of their range." I shoved my glasses up my nose. "The issue is redundancy. At the moment, each transmitter is carefully positioned to overlap. It's a safeguard to stop any dropouts in case one goes down."

"What do you need?" Jo asked, dipping her bread in her stew.

"Stuff Farmer doesn't have."

Farmer nodded from his seat at the head of the table. Mari sat on his lap, his arms around his woman.

"We're working on getting the parts you listed—set ourselves up as a major relay station. But that shit doesn't happen overnight. I've sent men out, but they haven't returned yet."

Shield scratched his chin. "Damn. What's the failure rate?"

I shrugged. "I give it twenty-eight percent."

"That high?"

I bristled, crossing my arms over my chest as I narrowed my gaze on Shield.

"It's cobbled together parts that are then drilled onto whatever rickety building we can find to support them. They're then exposed to the weather, animals and whatever other being might stumble across it. You want perfection? Build a time machine and travel back to the before. Otherwise, this," I rapped my knuckles gently against the side of my head. "Is the best you've got."

Shield's lips quirked. "Noted. But that doesn't solve our issues in the now." He frowned as he glanced back at the map. "The only other option is to go back the way we came. But I'm loathed to do that. No one—not even our nomads—should be travelling that path. Between the bastards and the migrant crowds, it's too dangerous."

My brain kicked into gear, rapidly searching for alternatives.

"Audrey?" Jo asked, laying a hand on my shoulder. "What are you thinking?"

I closed my eyes, the scenarios playing across the backs of my eyelids. Numbers trickled through my head, calculations of time, distance, speed, and weather.

I knew this wasn't normal. This was a skill few people possessed. I'd been described as gifted, a genius, a prodigy. The labels were bestowed on me by people who didn't understand how I did what I did. They were given to me by people who wanted to flatter and praise and use my skills for themselves.

My favourite labels, the ones I cared about, were daughter, sister, grandchild. They were the labels assigned to me in love and without judgement. There were no expectations placed upon me. No demands. Just acceptance.

Until there wasn't.

I blinked my eyes open, refocusing on the map.

"There are three possible options. The first is as Shield directed," I said, running my finger over the lines on the map.

"We divide our small group again and send some of the men to install the equipment along the route. It'll connect Cunnamulla to Farmer and down to Adaminaby. Once switched on, we'll have a direct line."

"But?" Lottie asked, flicking a curl away from her tired face. "I can sense a 'but' coming."

"But," I agreed, tapping a finger against the map. "The risks are significant. First, there's a higher chance of failure. Greater risk to our people, greater risk of the transmitters being discovered. It would also mean that if you want your nomads to be able to use the network, they'd have to travel along those roads—at least until we can expand it out further. Greater risk overall."

"Not a fan of splitting the group again," Butcher murmured from his spot beside me. "We've already sent Ghost and Ava on a wild goose chase to find your missing friends. Would be a damned shame to do the same again."

"Ghost can hold his own," Pope said, rocking back in his

chair, his hands clasped behind his head. "And my money is on the she-devil every time."

"That she-devil," Lottie said, shooting him an evil look. "Is my sister. But I concur."

"Back to the other options," I said, vaguely annoyed at being interrupted. "Option two is status quo. We run the transmitters on the new route using the same existing setup. We'll run short, but when we get to Cunnamulla, I can build new ones. We then backtrack or send some of the nomads to plant the missing signals. It'll take longer and add a few weeks to our plans, but it'll be safer in the long run." I glanced up, noting the expressions around the table.

"And the last option?" Shield asked, his gaze trained on me.

"We push the equipment to the edge and pray it's enough until we can add additional transmitters to bolster the signal." I tapped my finger along the new route. "Overlapping the transmitters presents less risk of failure. Not to mention routing them through a desert-like environment presents its own challenges."

Shield leaned back. "And there aren't any more options?"

I shook my head. "Not unless I can create a satellite and launch it within the next twenty-four hours."

A shadow of a smile touched his lips. "And you're sure you can't do that?"

I smiled. "Even I have limitations."

"Alright. Thoughts?"

"I vote for option three." Pope nodded at me. "Audrey wouldn't have suggested it if she didn't think it was a viable option."

"It is viable, but the risks are greater."

"Option one would be better, quicker, easier. And I could go," Switch offered, leaning across the table. "I know how to install them. If it's just me, there's less risk of being caught by The Purge or anyone else."

"I appreciate the enthusiasm," Shield said, shaking his head. "But I'm not supporting a suicide mission. I've ridden through that area and only came out of it alive by the skin of my teeth. You'd not only need to take a vehicle to transport the equipment, you'd also have to put yourself in danger getting out and installing without anyone to have your back." Shield shook his head again. "No, option one is off the table."

"Which leaves the other two." Runner played with Ellie's hair absently, his gaze unfocused. "We either hope for the best or end up in a situation no different to what we have now."

I watched Shield silently as the discussion went around and around. He allowed each person to say their peace, to feel as if they were being listened to and their opinion respected. But slowly, skilfully, he guided them to his preference. He led them through gentle questioning, prompting, through teasing and nods. He weighed and listened, but this conversation had been over before it already began.

It was mastery in motion. Perfected persuasion.

I couldn't withhold my admiration.

"You've already decided," I blurted out as the conversation began to wind up.

Shield's eyebrows rose. "Why do you say that?"

"Am I wrong?"

His lips twitched. "No, you're right. Option three makes the most sense. If it works, we get the benefits. If it doesn't, then we're no worse off than we already are."

It was the same option I'd have chosen—and the most obvious.

Jo sighed heavily, shoving to her feet. "So this all this

debate could have been saved by Audrey simply telling us the best option and Shield agreeing with her." She shook her head, her short hair flicking against her cheeks. "I'm going to bed. See you useless idiots tomorrow."

She began to stride away, halting at Texas' call.

"Sweet dreams, beautiful Jo. Be sure to dream of me."

She tossed him a glare over her shoulder. "Anything featuring you is a fucking nightmare."

He chuckled as she stormed out, pushing to his feet. "The lady doth protest too much."

"Does she?" Shield asked lightly. "Or do you need to back off?"

Texas paused, his amusement fading. "You know I wouldn't if she didn't enjoy it."

I watched, fascinated as Shield considered his brother.

"Make sure you keep it that way," he said finally.

Texas nodded once before his expression faded into amusement once more. "Should I stay up waiting at the door to make sure you get our girl home, okay?" he asked, dipping his head in my direction. "Her curfew is midnight, you know."

I knew Texas was teasing, but there was an undercurrent to his words, a kind of steel that implied he had my back even against his own President.

My insides felt strange at that. Kind of warm and gooey —but not at all unpleasant.

An arm looped around my shoulders, the touch casual and slightly possessive.

Pope.

"Our little sis needs her beauty rest," he told Shield, wagging a finger in his direction. "And don't be thinking for one second that just because you're the President, we wouldn't throw down for her."

I found myself strangely bereft of words. I had assumed they, at best, viewed me as a useful oddity and, at worst, a necessary annoyance.

I glanced around the table to see the men I'd ridden alongside the last few months nodding.

"Do you like me?" I blurted out, unable to decipher exactly what was happening.

Wrath's eyebrows raised. "What kind of question is that?" he asked, glancing from me to Kate. "Why the fuck would she think we didn't like her?"

Kate lifted one shoulder in a half-shrug. "Perhaps because you men don't express your affection as freely as we do."

"What are you talking about?" Pope demanded, hauling me closer to him. "I express my emotions just fine."

He ruffled my hair, giving me what I could only assume was meant to be a brotherly noogie.

"You can stop." I shoved his hand away, smoothing back my hair. "I think I understand now."

"Audrey." I glanced at Runner, who sat at the table, Ellie in his lap. "You're one of us. You're a valued member of this team. You're Club. That makes you family."

I swallowed, not at all comforted by his words.

Shield rose from his seat, his hand held out for me to take.

"I'll have her back by midnight," he promised, a twinkle in his eyes. "But don't wait up."

Pope gave me a little shove in his President's direction. "Have fun."

I took Shield's offered hand, tilting my head back to look up and him, searching his face. "Are we about to have sex?"

I heard snorts of amusement from the table behind me.

"No, honey. We're going for a walk."

My face fell, my bottom lip poking out. "That's a shame."

Shield chuckled, tugging me into his side. "I'm sorry my company pales in comparison to my sexual prowess."

I lifted a hand in farewell as he guided me around the table and outside.

The night air retained a little heat, a sultry tone that hinted at the coming summer months. Lamps lit various areas of the courtyard as men and women hung together in clumps, standing near barrels of fire or sitting on benches chatting as they worked.

It was a return to a time before television, when entertainment came from stories and conversation rather than performance, and there was always something to be done in the After. Mending, building, sorting—our days were full of movement and busy work, the kind of work that may not seem essential, butbecame so when you needed rope or sharp tools in a hurry.

"Where are you taking me?" I asked, following Shield to the edge of the wall.

He took my hand, pressing a kiss to my knuckles. "Do you trust me?"

I nodded.

"Then follow me."

9

SHIELD

The Labyrinth was a series of interconnected spaces that made up the internal parts of the wall surrounding Farmer's fortress. Purposefully built to slow down anyone who managed to breach their defences, I guided Audrey through the winding, twisting maze and up to a flight of stairs.

We ascended the steep staircase, my hand on her back, our bodies brushing together.

"How did you know I'd made my mind up?" I asked, listening to her small panting breaths as we climbed.

She shrugged. "Sometimes I just know things."

"Like?"

She stopped on the stairs, glancing at me over her shoulder. "I knew that Wrath and Kate wanted to be together long before they admitted it. I know that Runner makes Ellie happy, but she struggles to believe she's worth it sometimes. I know that Lottie is breaking herself to try and save Zero because she couldn't save someone in her life that she loved. I know that Butcher is hiding something. I know that Pope has a depth to him that he masks in an effort to keep people at bay. I know you—" she twisted, reaching out to brush fingers across my cheek. "Love your sister, but you both share a grief that even your joy at being reunited couldn't hide." Her knowing gaze searched mine. "I'm not good at relationships. I don't understand the dynamics when I'm in them. Words confuse me because they're often at odds with what someone is telegraphing through their behaviour. I'm excellent at observation. I thrive being on the sidelines."

"Being on the sideline isn't where I want you." I stepped closer, the stairs compensating for the differences in our height. "You're not a wallflower, Audrey. You're a hothouse bloom. You deserve to be praised, admired, and most of all, cared for."

Her eyes narrowed. "I don't want to be either of those."

My lips quirked. "No? What do you want to be then?"

"A useful plant, like a herb or a flower. Or, specifically, chamomile."

I swallowed a chuckle. "Go on."

She spoke with her hands, her long slender fingers dancing through the air as she explained her reasoning.

"I want to be useful. Helpful. Chamomile is an incredibly useful plant. It can be brewed to help with fevers, allergies, inflammation, menstrual pain, insomnia, wounds—the list goes on." Her hands dropped to her sides. "If you must compare me to a rose, tell me I am chamomile."

I leaned in, crowding her space.

"You're a constant surprise."

She flushed, dropping her gaze. "I know. People tell me that all the time."

I captured her chin with my hand, gently raising her head until our gazes met. "It's not a bad thing. Not at all."

Her brow furrowed, her nose wrinkling. "Are you kidding with me?"

I shook my head. "Never. Not about this."

"But—" she seemed at a loss for words. "Don't I annoy you?"

My lips quirked. "Not so far."

Her mouth slid open, her eyes wide behind her thick-rimmed glasses.

Unable to resist the temptation, I took advantage, leaning forward to kiss her.

Just as I had expected, Audrey ignited. Her arms wrapped around my neck, her body swaying to press against mine. She murmured something against my lips.

"What?" I asked, dropping my head from her mouth to press hot nips along her neck.

"I... I don't remember."

My growl filled the tight space. "Good."

I shifted us until her back pressed against the rough wall of the stairwell. With one hand, I encircled her wrists, yanking her hands above her head.

"Hold them there."

She stared at me with wide eyes, but did as I said, her small breasts heaving with gasping, excited breaths.

Gently I removed her glasses, folding the arms down before tucking them in my back pocket.

"Why would you—?"

I cupped her head, brushing my thumb against the apple of her cheek. " Selfish prick that I am, I want all your attention on me."

I returned to her mouth before she could protest or ask further questions. I wanted her curiosity focused on me. I wanted to tap into her insatiable thirst for knowledge to show her exactly how good it could be between us. I wanted her to explore her limits and embrace the experiences I was more than willing to give her.

Her greedy mouth responded to my kiss, her lips open-ing, allowing me to taste her pleading whimpers and breathy moans as we kissed.

Gently loosening my grip on her wrists, I slipped my hands down her arms, pleased as fuck when she kept her hands in place.

Her body fully at my leisure, I dug one hand into the silky strands of her hair while slipping the other around her middle and glided it down to palm her ass.

She made a little mew of pleasure, arching into me as if begging for more.

"Good girl," I murmured against her mouth. "Focus on me, Audrey. Focus on how I make you feel."

Determined to ensure her attention remained on me, I began to dance light caresses over her ass and tug gently on her hair.

I danced kisses across her cheek and up her jaw to her earlobe. Dragging my teeth down the sensitive skin, I relished her shudder as I nipped, then sucked to soothe the sting away.

Like any good general, I'd strategized my offensive, determined to overwhelm her with a myriad of sensations all geared toward quieting her mind and keeping her in this moment.

"What do I feel like against you?" I asked, my breath dancing against the shell of her ear. "Describe my touch."

"Hot," she whispered, her voice breathy and full of need. "Big. Overwhelming."

I sucked her earlobe into my mouth, grazing my tongue over the skin before letting it go once more. "Good over-whelming?"

"Yes." Her breathy response pulled at my cock. "Very good."

"Describe how good."

Her eyelids fluttered for a moment, then settled shut, her head tipping back to grant me access to her neck as I began to slowly, painfully slowly, kiss my way down to her collarbone.

"My labia is pulsing," she whispered, her voice stuttering, as if unsure of what to say or how to say it. "My underwear is distracting me."

I chuckled. "And why would that be?"

"The material is wet," she admitted, her skin warming with a flush under my lips. "I want you to remove them and take this deep, throbbing ache away."

Huffing out a quiet laugh at how badly this plan had backfired, I forced myself to pull away. Audrey's descriptions had sent my own arousal into overdrive.

I tugged her hands down, determined to ignore my frustrated dick.

"Follow me."

She blinked, a frown marring her brow as she slipped her hand into mine. "Did I say something wrong?"

"No, baby. We're just moving somewhere more comfortable."

Seemingly satisfied with my answer, she followed as I led her up the stairs and out onto the wall walkway. Weapons lined the wood, stone and steel fencing a stark reminder of the world in which we now lived.

Farmer had improved the fortifications since the last time I'd been here—more steel, more reinforced structures, more weapons. I didn't blame him. The After had become unpredictable, unexpected. Militia, cannibals, even slavery wasn't outside the realm of possibility and probability.

I doubt anyone predicted the mutation of humans into gnashing claws and gashing teethed bastards.

My Club needed protection, and I was doing everything within my power to ensure my people were safe. It killed me that Farmer wouldn't let me help him, and that my own sister's protection remained the responsibility of another man.

"This view is amazing," Audrey said. She stepped out onto the wall beside me, her head tilting back to look up at the stars.

THERE WERE no lights from cities to dim the spectacular view of the glittering milky way. The rich black skies seemed to be filled with a million shades of colour as the light from the crescent moon shone down upon us, glinting across her ebony hair.

Audrey lifted a hand to trace the constellations with her finger.

"My favourite is Dorado."

I GLANCED UP, unable to pick out shapes or shimmers in the vast sky.

"Why that one?"

Audrey grinned, her teeth flashing in the night. "It's home to the Tarantula Nebula, which is the most luminous nebula of its kind in the local universe. It spans thousands of light years from end to end. The Tarantula Nebula is an active star-forming nebula. It's the place where you can see stars being born."

I glanced back up to the sky, trying to imagine what that would look like.

Audrey sighed, tilting her head back as she gazed up at the sky. "Whenever I get stuck in my head or become broken by the trauma we're all experiencing every day, I look to Dorado. There's a comfort in knowing that my lifetime is less than a heartbeat in the history of the universe."

"Don't you feel insignificant?"

She snorted. "How can you feel insignificant when you're alive? Our lives may be a blink in time, but they are meaningful. We're part of the tapestry that is the history of our world, our society, our being. How can you feel insignificant when you are a part of the continuum?"

Unable to resist this incredible woman, I gave into temptation, capturing her hand, I tugged Audrey into my chest to press kiss after kiss against her eager lips. Drowning in her taste, in her scent, in the need that surged through my veins as I captured her, determined to brand myself upon her, to claim this woman as mine.

SHE WAS SO WHOLLY unlike any person I'd ever known. Confident in what she wanted and unabashedly afraid of stating her needs. Her brain worked in a myriad of mysterious ways, each more brilliant and unexpectedly delightful.

I wanted to unfurl her secrets, to unwrap her like a chocolate and savour every inch as I tasted my way across her body.

BUT FOR NOW, without a decent bed and no privacy I'd do as she requested and lick the sweet cream from between her legs.

RELUCTANTLY, I pulled away, covering her face and holding her close.

"Come," I whispered, relishing the unfocused look in her eyes. "Follow me."

I led her across the walkway toward one of the turrets on the rear wall and stepped inside, finding it empty.

Everyone took shifts, watching for bastards and other threats. But with dinner laid out below, the shifts were split, meaning every second tower was unmanned until later in the evening.

INSIDE THE CRUDE PLATFORM HOUSING, weapons decorated the walls—sniper rifles and handguns, a machine gun, a rocket launcher, extra cartridges of ammunition, knives and a long spear-like sword.

Audrey touched the handle of the sword, her expression thoughtful as I pulled a blank blanket from a box.

"What came first, do you think?" she asked, her thumb grazing the wood. "The weapons used for fighting or for hunting?"

I spread the blanket across the floor and eased down, my back to the wood wall.

"You tell me."

She shot me a grin. "I can't transport myself back thirty-million years."

"No?" I chuckled. "It appears we've discovered something you can't do."

She smiled, coming to sit down beside me. I shifted, making room for her as she settled.

"Do you ever wonder why we continue to perpetuate violence?"

My eyebrows rose. "Does it go beyond that we're all driven by an intrinsic need to survive?"

She frowned, her lips pursing together. "It's more than

that, isn't it? It's jealousy and rage, it's coveting what others have."

I settled in, fascinated by her thought process.

"Like the original sins?"

She made a noise. "I don't believe in organised religion."

"Fair enough. But that doesn't mean that the stories aren't important. They tell the shape of our history. Mythology is filled with moral messages."

Audrey tipped her head to one side, her eyes wide behind her glasses. "That's true. Though morality itself is often defined by those in power. It is inherently patriarchal."

I grinned. "Perhaps. But it doesn't have to be. Not anymore."

"Why were you upset when you saw Mari?"

The abrupt change in topic had me blinking. "Sorry?"

"Earlier. When you first greeted Mari. You both went from pleasure to pain. There was a melancholy feel to your interactions, a grief that pervaded your reunion."

Note to self, Audrey has superpowers.

I swallowed. "We have a younger sister—Harpa. She was in New York visiting our maternal grandmother when the virus started spreading. I told her to wait it out—I didn't want her travelling."

I glanced away, staring out into the night as I remembered those first dark days. The uncertainty, the misinformation, the fear.

"Two years she was stuck there. Two fucking years."

Audrey laid a hand on my arm. "Did she die?"

I shook my head. "No idea. After begging, bribing and threatening the consulate for two years, we managed to get her and our grandmother on a plane back home. Then the day they were due to fly out, the US government shut the

borders. Within forty-eight hours, the Australian government enacted the Dark."

The Dark had been the moment everything changed. In
the space of a few hours, every telecommunications option
had been rendered useless. The world had effectively
ended.

And with it, my hopes of ever seeing my sister again.

Audrey sucked in a breath. "Was that the last day you
spoke to her?"

I nodded.

"I'm sorry."

"Thank you."

We were silent for a moment, both of us lost to our
thoughts.

"I lost my family," Audrey murmured, her voice toneless
and devoid of emotions. "They fell in the first wave. One
after another. I told them to be careful. To isolate from each
other. We didn't know enough about the virus." She glanced
down at her lap, forcibly relaxing her clenched hands. "My
sister contracted it first. She was a doctor. Within twenty-
four hours, my mother had it, then my grandparents, my
father, and finally my brother." She sucked in a breath. "I
was a state away—it's what saved me."

And then you were alone.

I didn't say the words aloud, instead allowing them to lie
between us like a shadow, afraid she'd shatter if I gave the
spectre life.

"Do you think she's gone?"

I shook my head. "Harpa is strong. She's resilient. I know
the odds are against her, but I have to hope that she's not
just alive, but thriving—where ever she is."

We were silent for another beat.

"Perhaps all the stories are wrong," Audrey murmured.

"Perhaps survival at all costs is the only lesson in morality we need."

I brushed a hand across her cheek, capturing the loose strands of her damp hair with my fingers and tucking them behind her ear.

"You don't believe that."

"Don't I?" Her lips twisted into a self-deprecating smile. "I'm not sure what I believe anymore."

I caught her hand, lifting it to my lips and pressing a caress against her knuckles. "Then believe this," I murmured. "Even in the struggle, each of us is capable of greatness, Audrey. Each day when I wake, I look for the good. Our society ended, but our lives, our community, our humanity didn't. There's joy despite the struggle, just as there is joy *in* the struggle."

"There's joy in the struggle?"

"Would you like an example?" I grazed another kiss across her knuckles. "We struggle each day, and yet I find joy in the taste of your skin."

She stared at me, her eyes flicking across my face. "Shield?"

"Yes?"

"Kiss me."

I chuckled, my hand moving to cup the back of her head. "As you wish."

I kissed her—but softly this time, determined to slow us down and savour every breath. Audrey made a mew of surprise, then sank into me, her body twisting until she could plant a hand on my chest, bracing herself against me.

I teased her with long, gentle kisses that hinted at deeper, darker needs.

I drew back. "Lay down, baby," I said, guiding her with a hand to her back.

She complied, and I murmured my appreciation as I took her in, considering my plan of attack.

Savour her.

I dipped my head to press kisses along her neck, slipping my hands under her shirt to glide across her soft skin.

"Fast is better," Audrey murmured, tipping her head to grant me better access. "Less time to think."

I paused. "You shouldn't be thinking of anything, but me." I shifted to capture her mouth, our tongues dancing together in hot, hungry kisses. "Now, start describing what I'm doing to you."

Her breath caught. "It won't work."

"No?" I hummed. "Guess I better up my game."

"Shield—"

"Close your eyes, Audrey. And start describing."

She stared at me for a beat, her expression uncertain. Then slowly, ever so slowly, her eyelids drifted closed.

"Good girl." I rewarded her by slipping my hands under her back to unbuckle her bra. "Let's get you out of these clothes."

With deliberately brisk movements, I stripped her until all she wore were her glasses and a cloud of unease.

"Breathe," I whispered against the shell of her ear, relishing her shiver. "Just feel and describe."

I danced fingers slowly up and down her rib cage, listening to her breathing and pausing to retrace areas that seemed particularly sensitive.

"Tell me."

She sighed, her eyes still closed. "It feels... ticklish but soothing. "

I dipped my head, my mouth closing over the nipple of her left breast.

"Yes," Audrey hissed, fingers burrowing into my hair. "Hot. Wet."

I grazed my teeth against her nipple.

"Oh!" She arched, pushing her small breast into my face. "More."

Chuckling, I laved her nipple again, my thumb rubbing against her poorly neglected right breast.

Don't worry, honey. I'll get to you shortly.

"Shield... please."

I growled. "Please, what, Audrey? What do you want?"

She blinked her eyes open, seemingly lost for words.

"Want?" she repeated slowly. "Isn't it obvious?"

"Tell me, honey."

Her hand pressed against my head. "I want you to do that, but on my clitoris."

Chuckling, I resisted the pressure she applied. "Let me finish worshipping your breasts, then I'll go take care of your greedy pussy."

"Greedy pussy?" Her nose wrinkled. "Is that what I have?"

Holding in my chuckle, I bent my head to draw her right breast. "We'll see, won't we?"

I tasted her, flicking her nipple with my tongue as she squirmed under me, desperate little noises escaping her.

Slowly, I glided a hand up from her breast over her collarbone to wrap around her throat.

Audrey fell still, her pulse fluttering wildly under my thumb.

"What are you doing?" she asked.

"Keeping you in the moment." I planned on plying her with new sensations and unexpected actions, allowing no time for her mind to wander. "Say 'Red' if there's anything you hate or you want me to stop. If you can't verbalise it, tap on me twice, like this." I showed her with my free hand, curling it into a fist and tapping it gently against my sternum.

"Will we be doing things that require a safe word?"

I grinned. "Yes."

She blinked once, her eyes big behind her glasses. "Okay."

"Any more questions, or can I return to your gorgeous breasts?"

Audrey closed her eyes, tilting her head back. "You may resume the debauchery."

Chuckling, I lowered my head once more. This time I alternated sensation between her breasts, kissing one gently while rolling her opposite nipple, only to soothe the sweet ache with my tongue a moment later. I kept my hand where I was, wrapped around her neck—no pressure, just the weight and heat of it against her skin as I felt her pulse under my palm.

Shifting over her, I moved until I could reach between us to cup her mound. I danced my fingers across her sensitive skin, gratified to find her wet and hot.

Audrey whimpered as my finger parted her, dragging through her slick heat to find her clit.

"Fantastic," she groaned, her hips pressing up. "More."

Unable to fight temptation any longer. I reared back, ignoring her protest.

"Hush," I ordered, moving her until I was settled between her legs. "I'm about to memorise your taste."

Gripping her legs, I dove straight for the promised land without any hesitation. On another night, there would be soft kisses and drawn-out teasing along her legs and inner thighs, but tonight I needed her taste on my tongue.

I licked into her, parting her sweet folds and groaning at

the delicious taste of her on my tongue. This woman could quickly become my addiction.

I teased her, dancing around her clit, testing pressure and pattern, working out what drew her most ardent responses.

"Shield!" She gasped, rocking up then settling back down as I circled to the right of her clit.

"Fuck, Audrey. You're so wet. I can't wait to taste you coming. You gonna cum for me, pretty girl? You gonna be a good girl for me?"

She nodded, her lips moving, but no words escaped.

Pleased as fuck, I dropped my head, my tongue and lips gentle, but demanding as I forced moans and whimpers from Audrey's hot body.

"Harder," she whispered. "Please."

"Good girl," praising her, I renewed my efforts, gratified when her body bowed. Another beat, and her legs clenched around my head to cut off my circulation.

Fuck yes!

"Shield!"

Audrey broke, crying out with the force of her orgasm.

Swapping tongue for fingers, moving up her body, pressing hot, gasping kisses to her heated skin. Our lips met mine, and I forced her to lip her taste from my mouth, burning when she purred at the taste.

"That was...." She sighed, resting her head against my shoulder. "What I was hoping for."

Her admission added fuel to the fire already burning in my gut. I wanted to be in her. Needed to seat myself deep within her greedy pussy. That I was fully clothed while she remained naked under me was a goddamned travesty.

As if reading my thoughts, Audrey plucked at my shirt. "You're still dressed."

"So I am." I shifted back. "Take off my clothes."

Her eyes flashed in the dim light. "Are we going to have sex?"

"Not yet." I cupped her breasts. "But I am going to cum all over these pretty tits."

Her mouth parted in an 'oh' of surprise, and I took advantage, kissing her deeply.

"Shirt off," I barked between kisses.

Her fingers fumbled at my hem, capturing the material and tugging it up and over my head. Tossing it to the side, Audrey's hands dropped to my jeans, working the fly.

Pushing my jeans down, my cock—already rigid and aching—fell into her waiting hand.

"Oh." Audrey broke our kiss, shifting under me until she could see my dick. "Oh wow."

I swallowed my laughter. "Wow?"

She nodded, licking her lips. "Your cock is statistically on the average size for length. But thickness?" She glanced up at me, her gaze hot. "I'd place you in the upper ten percentile."

"And that's good?"

"Very." Her hand ran over my cock, firm and confident. "Thickness is very important. A vagina, when aroused, is only about four inches in length, so a longer cock isn't necessarily preferable to one with a circumference that will fill you up and stretch you out and hit all your erogenous zones while doing so."

She stroked my dick. "And you have the perfect circumference."

I never thought I'd be turned on while getting an education about sex organs. But here we were. Somehow Audrey made this hot as fuck.

Doesn't hurt she looks like a sexy professor.

"Were you a teacher in the Before?" I asked, imagining bending her over a desk.

"How did you know?"

Groaning, I thrust into her hand. "Fuck me." Gathering her in my arms, I rolled us until she was on top, straddling my hips.

"Here's what we're gonna do." I gripped her thighs, holding her wet pussy against my stomach. "You're gonna turn around and sit that hot cunt on my face. I'm gonna eat you out while you jerk me off. I'll come over your tits, we'll clean you up, then we're gonna have a little sleep and do it all over again. Got me?"

A slight flush coloured her cheeks. "Yes."

"Good." I spanked her ass. "Now give me your pussy."

Certain things drove me crazy in bed. The way a woman's back arched when she came. The dimples at the bottom of her spine. The scent of her arousal as I ate her out.

And fuck me if Audrey didn't hit every one of my trigger points.

She settled over me, her sweet cunt in my face.

"Good girl," I growled, hooking my arms around her thighs and hauling her back. "Now jerk me."

I devoured her pussy, licking and sucking with the frantic need of a ravenous wolf. Audrey cried out, her hips flexing as she began to ride my tongue.

I grazed a hand over her back, encouraging her to take what she wanted. I heard her spit then her hand tightened around my cock, using her saliva as lube.

The fuck if that didn't drive me wild. Shifting, I worked a hand between us, circling her opening with light, glancing touches. Her hips stilled, her hand on my cock losing its rhythm.

Good girl.

Slipping a finger into her cunt, I groaned against her, desperate to feel her tight muscles squeezing my dick as she screamed her release.

Hold it together.

I pumped my finger in and out, my mouth devouring her clit as I searched for the spot that would drive her wild.

As if on cue, Audrey gasped, rocking up then back, her hand on my dick squeezing tight.

Found you.

I worked her g-spot as she worked me, determined to tip her over the edge before I lost my self-control. Thank God Audrey was right there with me. With a strangled scream, she came, pulsing around my finger and flooding my face with her release. I guided her through, then rolled us until she was under me, panting and sated.

Slicking a hand through her wet spend, I gathered it, using it to jerk my cock in rough, brutal movements. Staring down at my gorgeous woman, it took an absurdly low number of strokes to push me over the edge. Jerking my dick, I painted her gorgeous breasts, relishing my mark on her.

Finally spent, I rolled off Audrey and lay beside her, catching my breath as I pulled her into my arms.

The silence between us stretched, companionable and easy. Finally, Audrey raised her head.

"Shield?"

"Mm?" I murmured, too exhausted to form words.

"Can we do that again?"

Chuckling, I pulled her into my chest. "Absolutely."

10

AUDREY

A hand clamped over my mouth, jolting me from sleep.

I blinked awake, tensing to protest, only to have the hand drop away.

"Hush," Shield whispered, his lips near my ear. "We have company. Listen."

A chill raced down my spine, the hairs on the back of my neck standing on end as I listened, taking in the unnatural silence of the night. In the distance I heard it, the rumble of something big and mechanical.

"Dress," Shield whispered. "If we can hear them, it means they aren't afraid of detection. And that means they have the gun power to back it up."

In silence, we dressed, my heart pounding as I began to consider scenarios, calculating our odds against as yet unknown threat.

There are only a few machines that make that kind of noise independently. This means we're either facing a tank or large engineering vehicles, or we're in for a fleet of mobile, weaponised militia.

"How close?" I asked, zipping up my jeans as Shield moved to the lookout, his gaze trained on the horizon.

"No lights," he murmured. "But the noise is growing. Best case, maybe an hour."

I nodded once as the door to the small tower pushed open. A man stood in the shadows, a sniper rifle in his hands. Average height, but strong and lean, his expression was grim as he entered the tower.

"Ryan," Shield greeted, pushing away from the lookout. "What's the plan?"

"We hold." He moved to Shield's side, beginning to set up the weapon. "But Audrey's needed downstairs."

I blinked. "What?"

"My wife is in labour, and Mari is precious cargo." Ryan glanced over. "Farmer says he needs you with them in case."

"Fuck."

I swallowed my own curse, echoing Shield's. A birth would complicate an already precarious situation.

"Audrey—" Shield stopped, scrubbing a hand over his face. "How much fuel do those tankers have?"

"Enough to get us to Cunnamulla and a little further. Why?"

"We might need to make a quick getaway."

A loud explosion in the distance cut off Shield's response, the wooden floor under our feet vibrating.

"They've made it to the landmines," Ryan commented mildly, his eye pressed to the scope of his rifle. "If they get past the pits, then we'll start to worry."

I glanced behind me, noting that all sources of light in the fort had been extinguished. Men and women hurried through the dark, weapons in hand, guided by the light of the moon.

In the distance, the mechanical roar stopped, the night falling silent.

"Shit," Shield murmured, placing a hand on my back. "Something's wrong."

Ryan flicked us an impatient look. "Get her down to the infirmary with the rest of the civvies and get your ass back here. We're gonna need all the help we can get."

Shield turned us, guiding me outside and pressing a hand between my shoulder blades. I crouched, keeping my body below the height of the wall to my right.

As we reached the staircase, a loud humming noise reached us. We both paused, exchanging a look in the dark.

"Is that a—?"

My question was cut off by a yell from the tower behind us.

"All down!"

Shield pushed me into the stairwell, pressing me against the wall as something whipped past the spot we'd been standing, covering the walkway.

"What is that?" I asked, my voice low and breathy.

"Camouflage netting," Shield murmured against the shell of my ear. "That noise? It's a helicopter. They know we're here."

Goosebumps rose on my skin, a chill skating down my back.

"Are we safe?"

Shield shifted, glancing up at the night sky through the canvas netting.

He didn't answer.

I shivered, wrapping my arms around myself as I began to run through the various possibilities and likelihoods, calculating our survival.

If they have a helicopter, that means they're military. Likely well equipped, well-fed, and well-resourced if their weaponry is still running. Fuel doesn't appear to be an issue, which means—

Shield caught my hand, tugging me into the stairwell and leading me down into the dark. He reached for weapons on the walls, handing them to me and tucking them in his clothes as we silently descended.

At the exit, he paused, his face tilting up as the helicopter drew closer, the noise terrifyingly loud in the silent night.

I wonder if this terror is how people felt when they first saw an airplane flying overhead. What could it be? What is that noise? What monster has come to devour us in our sleep?

Dust began to whip across the forecourt while people fled into doorways or hid under vehicles.

"Why are they doing that?" I asked, my voice raised.

"Night vision," Shield called back, sinking into the dark beside me.

The helicopter whipped overhead, shooting past our fortress, the power of its propeller sending equipment tumbling.

"Stay," Farmer called from somewhere within the forecourt as the noise began to recede. "They'll be back."

Shield slipped back inside, hitting a panel on one of the walls. It clicked open to reveal an ammunition closet, complete with sniper rifle and AK47.

He took the rifle, filling his pockets with spare rounds and loading the weapon.

"Audrey?" He crouched beside me as he began to check the weapon.

"Yes?"

Shield glanced up, his gaze piercing, his earlier warmth replaced by sharp, hard edges.

Here he is, the tried and tested leader. It's just as I thought. He

is a man of many faces—becoming that which you need, just as
you need it.

"When I say run," Shield said, adjusting his position.
"You go straight to the infirmary. In the surgery room there's
a large drain under the main bed. You pull that open and get
Mari, Ryan's wife, and your friends in there. Stay there until
Farmer, one of the brothers, or I come."

He jerked the weapon up, laying the butt against his
shoulder and pressing his eye to the scope.

"If we don't by morning, follow the drain pipe. There's a
latch on either side marked by three small dots. Pull the
latch and a trap door will open. Follow one of the tunnels—
doesn't matter which direction. They'll both take you ten
klicks in either direction to a safe house. In the barn you'll
find a map in the hayloft. The map will lead you to three
caches, including one with a stashed vehicle. Take it and go.
Get back to Adaminaby or up to Cunnamulla. But go. Don't
wait, don't play hero. You got me?"

I swallowed and nodded.

He spared me a glance. "Babe, I need you to say it."

"I understand."

"Good." He pressed his eye back against the scope. "You
have to keep them quiet. And the—" he hesitated. "The baby.
If these guys get in, they can't know you're here." He turned
his head, narrowing his gaze at me. "Promise me, Audrey."

"I promise."

A small amount of tension eased from his shoulders.

"Good." He turned back to glance up at the sky, the
sound of a helicopter increasing in the distance. "Here they
come."

I glanced out at the forecourt, a hand on the gun at my
hip. "What about the tankers? Shouldn't we move them?"

"Too late."

The helicopter flew overhead and looped back around, Shield braced, standing ready as it hovered above the compound, its bright spotlight swinging from one side of the fortress to the other.

They have the air advantage, but we have the element of surprise. If we can take down the helicopter outside of the fort, it'll begin to even the odds.

An idea took root, but before I could give it voice, a bright orange flare lit from the door of the helicopter then dropped, twirling through the air to fall on the netting. It burned for a moment, the netting catching fire before it fell through to light the courtyard.

"GET BACK!" Shield roared, throwing himself back and onto me.

The helicopter pulled away as I hit the ground, the breath knocking out of me.

"Wha—"

A force lifted us, rocking us across the floor to slam into the staircase, the world around us shuddering with the impact.

They bombed us!

A horrifying roar followed, the sound exploding in my ears until I could hear nothing.

The events hit one after another, flashes of light from the courtyard, explosions I could feel rattling in my bones and burning my skin—not no noise.

Unlike my body, my brain retained its capacity to function.

Body in shock. Lungs dazed. Temporarily deaf. Or permanently, I'm not sure yet. Skin experiencing heat flashing from the fire clouds. Shield is—Shield!

Shield had curled around me, holding tight as he fought

to protect me from the worst of the debris ricocheting through the entry.

I lifted my head, blinking past sweat—or was that blood?—to find him glaring down at me, his mouth moving even if I couldn't hear the words.

I grinned, touching a hand to his face as the explosions stopped rocking the structure around us, the earth under our bodies settling back into place.

It no sooner settled than he was on his feet, dragging me to a stand as he reached for his fallen weapon. Spinning me so we were face to face, he looked me over once—fast, then nodded. Pressing a hot, hard kiss to my lips, he ripped himself away, pointing in the direction of the infirmary.

I didn't have to be a lip reader to know what he was silently shouting.

Run!

I took off as he stepped from the safety of the staircase and lifted his weapon, pointing it up at the sky. The helicopter was gone; in its place was a giant orange glow on the other side of the wall.

Someone shot it down.

Heaving a breath into my bruised chest, I forced myself to sprint through shadows that danced along the imposing walls, dodging fiery debris, wounded animals, and smouldering harvest.

These monsters have no idea the bounty they're hell-bent on destroying.

A tinny ringing began in my ears as I swayed across the yard, jumping over an upturned barrel to run the last few metres to the infirmary. Shoving open a door, I wheeled back, my hands flying up to protect my face.

Jo lowered the gun, taking a step back. Her face was

pale, her eyes wide, her short hair standing on end as she stared at me then yanked me inside and slammed the door.

Her mouth moved, but I couldn't hear, her expression frantic as she pointed down the hall toward the surgery room. Around us, women crouched, some holding weapons, others huddled together in fearful packs.

I brushed through their midst, Jo at my back as I searched for familiar faces— Ellie, Kate, Mari, and Lottie.

Distantly, in the back of my mind, I heard the whisper.

This is why we don't do relationships, the voice hissed as I grew frantic, throwing open doors and jerking crouched women back to stare down at unfamiliar, tear-streaked faces.

If you don't care, you won't hurt.

My ears popped as I threw open the door of the surgery room, the sounds of gunfire and explosions fading away as relief hit me in the belly.

"Hold it!" Zero lay in a bed, the remaining stump of his arm heavily banded, while his other hand held a gun pointed at me with scary stillness. The biker was pale and sweating, his sunken eye surrounded by thick dark circles and yet that gun never wavered.

"Oh," he said, lowering it. "It's you."

I took in the scene with a glance, a lump of relief rising in my throat.

A woman stood in the middle of the room, bent over panting, as she groaned through a contraction. Kate shot me a smile over the woman's head as she rubbed her back. "Good girl," she cooed. "Breathe through it. Not long now."

At the sink, Lottie, Mari and Ellie stood washing their hands, all of them staring at me.

"Thank the gods," Ellie whispered, tears shimmering in the dim light of the room. "You survived."

I swallowed the lump in my throat. "Just." I shoved my glasses up my nose, nodding at the woman. "Your baby has perfect timing."

A glimmer of a smile touched her lips. "It's definitely a boy."

"Ryan says hi." I grimaced as an explosion rocked our small building. "He's still alive."

Mari's smile slipped. "Did you see Farmer?"

Behind her, Kate made a face, giving me big eyes.

"Yes," I lied, hating the halting, awkward way the words fell from my lips. "He also says hi."

Mari wilted, falling against Ellie, her hands cupping her belly. "Thank God."

Please be alive, I begged the universe. *Don't let me be a liar.*

Lottie, looking pale and scared, finished washing her hands and turned away from the sink, approaching the other woman with a determined smile.

"Okay, Lindsay. We're gonna get you prepped now. This baby is coming, and I need to see what we're working with."

Average height with a shock of blonde hair, she bent in two, groaning through another contraction.

"Mother fucker," she muttered, her face red and sweat-stained. "This is just typical. A baby and a fucking war. Just what we need."

I grinned and stepped back, letting them fuss over her as my focus shifted to our next move.

"We need to open the drain," I said to Jo, pointing at the heavy metal in the centre of the room. "Shield says there's a way out down there."

Jo raised her eyebrow. "Convenient." She jerked a finger at the closed door behind her. "Do we take them with us?"

I bit my lip, rapidly calculating the risks. Before I could come up with a solution, Zero interrupted.

"No." He pushed up, struggling to rise from the bed. "We're fucked as it is. More people, more problems. I know they're your sisters or some shit, but we got a new mum, a pregnant woman, and a fucking cripple to deal with."

"Don't talk about yourself like that!" Lottie snapped, glaring at him as she and Mari supported Lindsay through another contraction. "That word is disgusting and in no way represents your ability or contribution to this world. Stop saying it."

Zero stared at her for a beat, then jerked his gaze away, looking back at me. "Lock the door and bar it. Let's get this thing lifted."

Heaving and struggling, Zero, Jo and I managed to wedge it up and drag it just enough across the floor to give us space to crawl in. Shining a light down, I could see that the giant pipe was surprisingly empty except for two small backpacks and a thin layer of dirt.

"How did you know?" Mari asked as we threw down the mattress from Zero's hospital bed.

"Shield." I glanced up, a wry smile twisting my lips. "And if you don't know about it, I'd say this was his Plan B if things went south with your husband."

Mari chuckled. "Sounds about right."

We lowered Lottie first, then Kate and Mari. With gentle hands, it took all of us to transfer Lindsay into the drain. Her contractions were streaming together now, the explosions and gunfire a high-paced theme song.

Jo hesitated at the lip, glancing back at the door.

"What?" I asked, watching Zero.

His head tipped to one side. "How do we get the grate back on?"

We both looked down at the heavy metal lid, a sinking feeling taking root in my belly.

One of us has to stay.

Zero huffed out a laugh. "Well fuck me." He crouched down, resting his ass against the lip. "Guess that's my signal.

"You can't," I protested, staring pointedly at his amputated limb. "It's too heavy."

"Audrey," he sighed, closing his eyes. "Shut the fuck up and let me pretend to be a man. Okay? If someone has to die a hero, at least let it be me."

"That's the most patriarchal self-aggrandising bullshit I've ever—" Jo began.

"Please." Zero glanced from me to Jo and back. "Let me do this."

With a shuddering breath, I took Jo's hand, pulling her away from the weakened man.

"Audrey, we can't. He's—"

I tugged her with me. "Made his choice." I glanced at him over my shoulder, giving him a final nod. "See you in a few hours."

A shadow of a smile pricked at his lips. "Look after the little doctor for me. She's sensitive."

And with that, we slipped into the drain and Zero slowly, haltingly sealed us in.

As the lid clicked into place, blocking the light, Kate switched on a torch, holding it up in the dark tunnel.

"Alright," she said, squeezing Lindsay's shoulder. "Let's get your baby delivered."

11

SHIELD

I stood on the wall of the fortress that protected the people I held dear and picked off the invaders one by one. They rushed the gate—fuckwits they were—expecting we'd be easy pickings. No doubt they'd done this to others, rushing their places at night, using their helicopter to terrorise.

No more.

I wasn't sure who took out the chopper, but I'd sure as hell be buying them a beer... if we made it out alive.

A call went up from the courtyard, rippling up the stairs and down the line.

"Farmer is down."

I glanced at Ryan, who stood calmly reloading his own rifle before picking off another target.

"You good here?" I asked.

"Go. I'll hold the line." He glanced at me. "And Shield? Make sure Lindsay's looked after."

I nodded. "Of course."

I darted across the open space, jumping over smouldering debris and dodging terrified livestock. Thick smoke choked the air, the acrid smell mixing with the sickly metallic bite of gunpowder and blood.

Death.

The smell had accompanied me through two tours of duty, the stench imprinted upon my soul. It seemed that even at the end of the world, I couldn't escape it.

I made it to the barn where Farmer had set up a makeshift headquarters. Injured men and women stood, guarding the area while they waited for attention. The small medical team made up of a doctor and two nurses worked on Farmer.

"Well shit," I muttered, dropping into a crouch beside the fucker. "Mari's gonna kill you now."

A ghost of a smile touched Farmer's lips. "Don't tell her. I'll be fine."

The fuck he will.

A piece of sheet metal had impeded itself deep in his abdomen. Dark blood poured from the wound, and in the shitty light of a few incandescent globes, I could see it ran black.

He can't die.

I gripped his hand, squeezing it tight. "What do you need?"

He closed his eyes, and that, more than anything, scared the fuck out of me.

"You'll have to lead. They'll listen to you. Keep them outside the walls. Worst case, get my people out." He blinked his eyes open as the doctor began to flush the wound. "And look after Mari. If I don't—"

"No takebacks," I interrupted, refusing to entertain the thought. "You took her, you're stuck with her for life. Which means you're gonna have to stay alive." I squeezed his hand one last time as the ground under us shook with the impact of another explosion. "See you soon, brother."

I pushed up from the ground, grabbing the sniper rifle and checking my ammunition as I assessed our options. We were outgunned and outmanned, but not down and out. The walls were holding, our people were well trained, and we had the height advantage."

"Prez?" Wrath fell in beside me. The guy looked like shit. Dirt and blood covered him in a thin layer of filth, blood leaking sluggishly from a cut on his cheek.

"Report?" I asked, ignoring Farmer's groan of pain behind us.

"They're suffering heavy casualties, but they're getting angry and desperate. They want in."

I frowned. "What's their play?"

"If I had to guess? Fire. They'll try to burn the place down."

I grimaced. The fortress Farmer had created was surrounded by farming fields and thick, dense brush. A fire would be devastating for everyone involved.

I considered our options, listening to the far too familiar sound of war.

"We need to act now," I decided, beginning to stride to the back of the barn. Wrath fell in beside me.

"What are you thinking?"

"We need to be proactive. Take them before they can take us." I clicked my fingers, pointing at the tankers that had—miraculously—survived any significant damage.

"You want to blow up our fuel?" Wrath asked, his eyebrows raising.

"No." A grin stretched across my face. "We're gonna make bombs."

Gunfire, shouts, and the occasional explosion became

background noise while Wrath and I worked to assemble a series of improvised explosive devices. Back in the service, we'd been forced to learn how to make them in order to know what to look for when dismantling them. Crude but effective, I hoped they'd be the turning point in this unexpected siege.

"Where are the brothers?" I asked as Wrath gently handed me his device.

"On the wall. Runner and Butcher are laying fire while Texas and Swift try to hit the vehicles."

I cocked an eyebrow in question.

"The explosions," Wrath said with a nod to where the chopper had gone down. "They found a rocket launcher and are putting it to good use."

I grinned. "Let's go give 'em a hand, shall we?"

Wrath led the way, clearing a path as I balanced the devices carefully in my arms.

One wrong step. One single jolt, and this could be game over.

On the wall we crouched, keeping our heads below the skyline as bullets whizzed overhead, bedding in the wood or ricocheting off the steel walls.

We scurried into the tower, finding Ryan, Runner and Butcher picking off targets.

"Boys," I greeted, gently placing my creations on the wood floor. "I come bearing gifts."

Ryan glanced over, grunting when he saw the canisters.

"Might work. These fuckers are persistent."

As if to prove his point, a grenade detonated against the fortress wall, rocking the tower.

"Fuck," Runner groaned, bracing himself as it swayed back into place. "Now I'm pissed."

I palmed one of the IEDs, checking the trigger. "Ready when you are."

Lifting a device, I stepped forward, assessing the battlefield as I picked my target.

The body count was high. Men lay dead or dying, strewn across the ground that ran wet with their blood. Body parts lay next to overturned vehicles while men cowered—their determination hanging on by a thread.

Snip, snip motherfuckers.

I tossed the IED into a cluster of armed soldiers pressing toward the gates. The device arched gracefully, falling amongst them.

"Shit. It didn't trigger." Butcher raised his rifle. "You want me to—"

The explosion blasted the enemy into the air, tossing bodies and ripping skin from bone. The heat from it hit us like a hot breeze in the middle of summer.

"Never mind."

Another toss of a second device and their lines shattered. Men panicked, running into the dense brush, while others gave up, laying weapons down to surrender.

"Orders?" Ryan asked, his eye glued to the scope.

I considered our options. We could let these fuckers go, send them running back to whatever hole they'd crawled out of and pray they didn't return with more firepower.

Or we could put them down.

All of them.

"Cull them." The words tasted like acid on my tongue. "We can't afford for word of this place to get out. Gather a team and hunt them down. All of them."

Ryan lifted, handing his position over to Wrath. "On it. How's Farmer?"

"Last I checked? Alive and whinging."

Ryan nodded once, then switched, a mask dropping over him. "Don't worry. We'll get them."

He called for men from across the wall—guys we'd both worked with while on tours of duty. Men used to hunting and dispatching those who would do us harm.

Only back then we'd fought to bring them to justice—bound by the rules of international warfare and our own morality.

Any morality I may have once possessed had corrupted long ago. Now I made choices based on one simple question—would it protect my people?

The decision to kill them—even those prepared to surrender—would mark my soul.

You've made your bed. Go fucking lie in the filth.

I clapped Butcher on the shoulder. "Where's Pope?"

He jerked his head toward the opposite side of the wall. "Watching our six. Fuckers tried to do a two-pronged attack. He and some of Farmer's guys took care of the rats."

Satisfied my people were safe for the time being, I collected my weapons. "Butcher, you're in charge. Runner, go check on Farmer. Wrath, there's a drain in the surgery room at the back of the infirmary. Our women are hiding there. Get them out and find out about Mari. Farmer's gonna want an update. Swift, start gathering the injured and get others to help. We need a triage tent. The infirmary isn't set up to cope with big numbers."

I glanced around at the carnage. "Alright. I'll see you soon."

Texas hit the trigger of his gun, taking down a man. "Where are you going?"

I pulled my handgun free, sliding off the safety. "Hunting."

12

AUDREY

"I can't!" Lindsay panted, a desperate keen sliding from between her clenched teeth.

"You can," Lottie praised, her head buried between Lindsay's knees. "The baby is nearly here, honey. You're so close. Two more pushes, and they'll be here. Just two more."

Ellie, Jo and I held her, supporting Lindsay's body as she strained and begged, desperately trying to smother her screams.

"You said that an hour ago!"

Lottie looked up with a tired grin, her face sweaty and deeply lined. The artificial white light of the camp lantern brought into stark relief the exhaustion that simmered beneath her surface.

"This time, I mean it."

I rubbed Lindsay's back, supporting her with my shoulders to keep her seated upright. Jo and Ellie crouched on either side, holding her hands and arms, equally supporting her weight. Behind Lottie stood Kate and Mari with clean blankets and various medical equipment laid out, ready to assist.

Another contraction gripped her, sweat pouring from her skin as she panted and groaned through the pain.

The promise of two pushes failed to come true as the baby, stubborn as a mule, remained inside.

"I can't," Lindsay sobbed, collapsing against me. "I-I c-c-can't."

Lottie opened her mouth, but Jo beat her to the punch. She cupped Lindsay's face and leaned in, her gaze catching and holding the pregnant woman's.

"You are doing your life's work," Jo said, her tone low and sharp. "You've provided a safe haven for your child. You've loved them without knowing them. You sheltered them with your body. You've protected them from harm. You're giving them life. Lindsay. Now bring them into this world. It's safe. It's warm. And you are supported. You have a safe harbour with us." She pressed her forehead against Lindsay's. "You can do this. This labour is as old as time. In some religions, they call this the women's curse. But it's not. It's a blessing. This is an experience only you can have. Each contraction is yours. It's your gift to give, Lindsay. It's your hard work that will bring this new life into the world."

She drew back, dropping her hands to clasp the woman's hand. "Push, honey. It's time to meet your daughter."

Who would have thought Jo was capable of such emotional eloquence?

"Shit," Mari whispered. "I want you as my midwife."

Lindsay drew in a shuddering breath as another contraction rippled through her body.

"I can do this," she whispered, holding Jo's gaze.

"Yeah, you can."

She closed her eyes, sucking in a breath. "I can do this."

"She's crowning," Lottie praised as Lindsay pushed.

Groaning low and long, she bore down, her baby caught by Lottie as she slid into the world.

Covered in blood, red and scrawny with a mop of dark hair, the baby remained soundless and motionless as Lottie began to work on the tiny body, rubbing her briskly and clearing her mouth and nasal passages.

My heart seized.

Don't die. Don't die. Don't die.

A tiny arm twitched.

Don't die. Don't die. Don't die.

The baby unravelled, her scrunched little body expanding as she sucked in air, opened her mouth and declared her place in this world.

Thank God.

Lindsay surged forward, her arms open. "Can I—"

"One second." Lottie cut the umbilical cord and tied it off, dapping it gently with iodine. Mari washed her little body with quick, efficient wipes, then handed her to Kate to wrap in a warm blanket.

Clean, healthy and wrapped up like a burrito, Kate placed the baby in her mother's waiting arms.

"Hello, Hope," Lindsay whispered, staring at her crying baby. "Happy birthday, little one."

The baby stopped, her tiny mouth opening and closing, her eyes scrunching as if she desperately wanted to open them to see her mother.

Does she know? I wondered, fascinated by this new life. *Is there some intangible bond that already exists between them? Or is this an evolutionary trait, a quirk of genetics that the pitch of a mother's voice calms the baby, implying love where none is yet to exist?*

I stepped back, allowing Jo and Kate to place the backpacks behind Lindsay, supporting her as she reclined with her child. Ellie crouched beside Lottie, helping to clear away the blood-stained medical sheets and gently wash the woman's legs and body.

I moved to help, only to be greeted by the afterbirth. It looked like squishy minced meat wrapped in a sausage filling.

Fascinated, I wanted to dissect it and understand the intricacies and indignities of this most sacred of events.

"Don't," Lottie said, slapping my hand. "You're not wearing gloves."

"Then give me some."

"Abso-fucking-lutely not."

I grunted, annoyed but not surprised.

Mari gagged, pressing a hand to her lips. "Jesus. That's rank."

"You'll have to push that out soon enough," I pointed out.

She wrinkled her nose. "Yeah, no. I think that this whole experience has proved that while a miracle, it's better to be ignorant of the grim realities."

Lottie chuckled. "Hard to put the reality back in the bottle once you've witnessed it." She stood, straightening with a groan.

"Are you okay?"

Deep bruises marred the veins on her arms—evidence of the blood she'd given to Zero.

"I'll be fine," she replied with a shadow of a smile. "Just need a good night's sleep and some food." She rubbed a tired hand across her face. "I wish I'd gone to medical school. A vet isn't as useful in the After as one would assume."

"No?" I gestured at Lindsay, who cooed adoringly to her baby. "Over ninety percent of doctors were infected by the virus. If you'd been a doctor, you might not be here." I took a chance, wrapping an arm around her shoulder and giving her a squeeze. "I'd say you've done well."

She sighed heavily, leaning into me. "If I knew more, I'd worry less."

I made a sound in the back of my throat. "No, you wouldn't. You're a worrier warrior, Lottie. And that is okay."

She smiled weakly and shifted. "The baby can probably start suckling now. Do you want to try?"

Lindsay nodded, adjusting her position on the mattress.

It took a few attempts before the baby latched on, her little rosebud mouth sucking frantically at Lindsay's breast.

I glanced at Jo. "How did you know it was a girl?"

Her lips twisted into a wry smile. "I didn't."

Silence descended, broken only by the low drone of the camp light and the soft suckling sounds of the newborn.

I jerked upright as awareness stole over me. "The fighting's stopped."

The room stilled as we all strained to hear the now familiar sound of explosions and gunfire.

"S-s-should we go see?" Kate asked.

I shook my head. "Shield said to stay until someone came."

And so we waited in a drain that smelled like blood and sweat for men who might be dead.

Just as my hope began to wane, the drain lid shook above us.

I grabbed my weapon as Jo stepped in front of Mari, her gun trained at the small gap.

"Hey? You guys still alive in there?"

Relief oozed the tension from my muscles.

"We're alive," Kate called to Wrath, her grin wide. "You okay?"

"Peachy," her man replied, grunting as he dragged the lid open wider. "Shit. There's a baby in here."

Lindsay grinned up at him tiredly. "Have you seen Ryan?"

"Yep. Fit as a fiddle. He's gonna be mad as hell he missed the birth."

"I'll hold it over his head forever," Lindsay promised.

"And Framer?" Mari asked, her hand pressed tight to her belly.

Wrath's hesitation was barely perceptible. "Not recently. Last I saw, he was ordering people around." He changed the subject. "How about we get you out of there?"

Wrath, Runner and Pope helped us out one at a time before jumping down to gently lift Mari, Lindsay and the baby.

They herded us through the infirmary, which was filled with injured people. Lottie stopped at the foot of Zero's bed where the man lay sleeping, my dog curled at the foot of his bed.

Killer wagged her tail once in greeting but remained where she was.

"Is he okay?" Lottie asked Runner.

"Yeah. Just exhausted. Waited up all night to make sure you guys were protected. Killer arrived from God knows where a little while ago. Can't seem to move her."

Lottie hesitated, then took a seat beside Zero's bed. "I'll stay here if that's alright?"

We left her, exiting the building into the aftermath of a war zone.

Bullet casings littered the yard that only hours earlier had felt like a pristine haven. Smouldering pieces of rubble sat here and there while livestock wandered around, snuffling through the burned remains of grain bins.

"Did they get in?" I asked, surprised to find my voice sounded loud in the hushed light of dawn.

"No, but they had decent weaponry to attack us."

As we walked across the foreyard towards the old homestead, I took note of the pock-marked walls and the gaping wounds in the otherwise solid wall. The men and women who'd fought sat in clumps seeing to their wounds tended or resting. Others patrolled the walls, their weapons at the ready.

"Where's Shield?" I asked, searching the faces of those around us.

"Out on the hunt." Pope glanced my way, his face closed and distant. "They'll be back—after."

I didn't dare consider what 'after' meant.

The carnage around us sent my primitive brain into a spiral. My anxiety began to peak as 'what ifs' hit me one after another.

What if they hadn't stopped them? What if the walls had fallen? What if... what if... what if...?

In the Before, if I was in a cycle of what-if-ery, I'd meditate or do things that made me feel safe. If I was really bad —and there were times that had happened—I'd book in with my psychologist, talking through different strategies to break the thought patterns.

Out here, nowhere was safe, and there sure as hell weren't places to meditate or psychologists to talk to.

"Audrey." Pope caught my arm, gently steering me away from a pile of clothing.

No. Not clothing. A body.

I sucked in a deep breath, turning my face away. The fingers on both my hands began to flick one at a time against my thumbs, the simple, rhythmic motion somehow soothing in amongst all this horror.

Pointer, middle, ring, pinkie. Pinkie, ring, middle, pointer.

Back and forth, back and forth.

Jo's hand slipped into mine, halting my movements.

"Breathe," she whispered, squeezing my hand as we approached the barn. "I've got you."

The barn had transformed from a headquarters into a triage centre. People were stretched out on makeshift mattresses or tucked into stalls as they attempted to patch animals.

My boot slipped in a puddle. I glanced down, bracing myself against a barn wall, only to find I'd stepped in a dark pool of blood.

Breathe. You've lived through the end of the world and the Purge attack. You've seen bastards and escaped a horde. You're capable of dealing with this. People need you, Audrey. You need to help.

Sucking in a breath, I straightened my shoulders and lifted my head.

Good girl. Now go be useful.

"Where's Farmer?" Mari asked, glancing around.

The men exchanged a glance over her head, and my heart seized.

Oh no.

"This way." Runner led us through the pack of people and down to the small tack room in the rear of the building. A doctor stood outside, shoulders slumped, clothes covered in blood.

"Phillip...?" Mari's voice waivered as she stared at the doctor. "Where is my husband?"

The doctor straightened, pushing off the wall. "Mari. I—"

Pale and exhausted, Mari straightened, her hands going to her hips. "Where is he?"

Phillip swallowed. "Mari, honey. Maybe we should—"

"In here?" She shoved the tack room door open and stepped through.

"Fuck," Runner grunted. "Mari, he's—"

A loud keening cry split the air, the sound pulled from the depth of hell itself.

My heart sank, grief stabbing me in the gut.

"Jesus, woman," a familiar voice grumbled. "Can't a man sleep?"

My head jerked up, the grief burning away.

"Is that—?" Kate laughed. "Holy shit. I thought...."

Pope shook his head. "Don't get your hopes up. He's in bad shape. Real bad. Fucking miracle he's made it this long. Just... be prepared."

Sobs of relief were undercut by soft murmurings. After a few beats of awkwardly standing around, Jo shook her head.

"Okay, let's give them some space. There are people who need help. Let's get to work."

I glanced at the doctor. "Is he gonna make it?"

A muscle jumped in his jaw. "You believe in God?"

I shook my head. "I believe in science."

"Then let's hope I have enough training to keep him alive."

I hesitated. "Is there something I can do to help?"

"Triage," he said, gesturing at the people around us. "Find those we can save. Triage them."

"And those we can't?"

He closed his eyes. "Make them comfortable."

I sucked in a breath, staring at the bloody ground while he moved on to his next patient.

You're best placed for this. This is what you do. It's statistics. It's logic. It's balancing the odds.

But I knew the decisions I was about to make would haunt me for the rest of my life.

13

SHIELD

I collapsed into the chair beside the hearth.

"You get them?" Pope asked, offering me a cut of water.

"Yeah." I gulped the liquid, grateful to clear the dust and guilt from my throat.

"Good." He held out a water jug. "More?"

I nodded. "Farmer?"

"Hanging in there. Stubborn bastard doesn't know how to quick."

Some of my worries eased.

"And Mari? The baby?"

Pope nodded behind my head. "See for yourself."

I twisted in my seat, a grin breaking across my filthy face. Dressed in a flowing yellow gown, Mari walked toward me, a bundle cradled in her arms.

Grief punched me, unexpected and unwelcome. The baby wasn't Mari's, I knew that, but I also knew that there was a good chance I wouldn't be here when she gave birth.

Yet another moment that the After would rob from me.

"And who is this?" I stood, holding my arms out to take

the baby. "Unless I've time jumped, I suspect she's not yours."

"Uh-uh, not until you're clean." Mari clucked. "But this is Hope. We're having a little walk while her parents sleep."

The baby yawned, blinking up at me with big blue eyes.

A lump the size of the moon stuck in my throat. I swallowed, then swallowed again.

Harpa's eyes had been this blue. Fuck I miss you, little sis. Be safe.

I bent, brushing my lips across the baby's soft head. "Hello, darlin'. Welcome to the world."

Such as it is.

Mari's gaze raked over me, her smile dimming. "You're exhausted."

"Three days of rough living will do that." I scrubbed a hand over my face. "Give me some food, a shower and bed." I caught her expression. "I'll be fine. Promise."

"I know." She forced a smile. "Farmer will be glad to hear you're home safe."

"Bet he's spitting mad at being laid up."

She chuckled. "He is. But he's getting better, and that's the main thing."

I bit my tongue to keep from tempering her hope. "That's good."

"Mind if I interrupt?"

I twisted to find Audrey holding out a bowl to me. "Hi."

"Hey." I drank her in, relieved to find her physically healthy. "Miss me?"

She grinned, shoving the glasses up her nose. "Maybe a little."

Hope began to fuss, pulling Mari's attention away. "Excuse me, I need to change her nappy."

"And you," Audrey said, handing me the bowl. "Should eat."

I took the offered food gratefully. "Sit with me?"

She flushed, glancing down at her feet. "Okay."

We sat at one of the long tables across from each other, Audrey as pretty as a picture and me covered in muck and mess.

She propped her chin on her hand, watching me eat.

"Would you call this a second date?" I asked, breaking our uncomfortable silence.

She grinned. "If it is, then our first date is one for the history books." She ticked off the events on her fingers. "Saved you from Bastards, propositioned you, made a cake for your pregnant sister, met the family, helped plan a telecommunications route, survived an invasion—what have I missed?"

"The epic oral?"

She laughed. "And epic oral sex."

I pretended to wipe my brow. "Phew. I was worried you weren't interested in seconds."

Her smile stuttered. "Do you... do you mean that?"

"Of course." I leaned in. "Why do you think I wouldn't?"

She shrugged. "I'm not exactly an easy lay."

"I'm not afraid of a challenge."

"Is that how you see me?" she asked, cocking an eyebrow. "As a challenge?"

I took a bite of the warm porridge she'd made for me, chewing thoughtfully.

"Not how you think," I said finally. "You're a puzzle. Whenever I think I have you figured out, you do something new and unexpected."

"You've known me for less than a week—and of that, you've not been in my company for three days." She tipped her head to one side. "I'm unclear on how you can solve the mystery of who a person is within that timeframe."

"That's because you're an individualist. You believe everyone is of intrinsic value and worthy of deep examination." I stabbed a strawberry piece with my fork, brandishing it to illustrate my point. "Me? I'm a realist. People are —for the most part—simple creatures. They're motivated by self-interest. Sure, some are better than that, but the majority aren't overly surprising."

Audrey pushed her glasses up her nose, frowning. "That's quite an indictment on your fellow humans."

"But am I wrong?"

She chuckled, leaning across the table to pluck a strawberry from my bowl. "No. It's why when I decided to set up our little colony, I ensured there were only women in our group. Men will listen to their ego over the truth, and children are too easily led astray." She made a face. "I know that sounds terrible, but I prioritised our survival at the time."

I nodded. "Did it mean you ruled anyone out?"

She shook her head.

"Then it's not terrible. It's sensible." I plucked a raspberry from my bowl and offered it to her. "You may not think it, but you're a leader."

She took the raspberry, chewing it thoughtfully.

"We're the people who make the hard decisions, babe. When shit gets real, we weigh up life and death." I huffed out a sigh. "People like to think we're the heroes, but we'll always be the villains."

"Because someone always gets hurt."

I met her gaze. "Yeah. Someone always gets hurt."

We fell silent as I finished my meal.

"The Doc told me what you did," I said quietly. "You okay?"

Her expression shuttered. "How was it hunting men?"

"Horrifying, I answered honestly. "I don't enjoy killing men who are just following orders."

"Ditto." There were shadows in her eyes. "I'll never know if I made the right choices. Deciding who lives and dies... if my decision sealed a fate that could have been prevented."

"No," I agreed. "But you did the best you could with the tools and knowledge you had at the time. It's all any of us can do."

She shuffled in her seat. "Can we change the subject?"

I allowed her a reprieve. "Sure."

"Are you still planning on going to Cunnamulla?"

I nodded at her question. "My people need me."

Her eyes flashed. "Which means Mari gets hurt."

"Yeah. Being the one in charge is a bastard."

She tapped her fingers against the tabletop. "No one sees me as a leader."

"No?" I pushed my chair back and stood. "Then why do they make decisions based on your advice?"

She blinked. "But that's not being in charge."

"Isn't it?"

She seemed to be at a loss for words.

"Come on." I picked up my bowl. "I need a shower, and you need to get to work."

She stood slowly. "Doing what?"

"Me."

14

AUDREY

Shield, it appeared, had a thing for playing in the shower. I wasn't yet sure if it was the illicitness of sex in a semi-public place or if he was a fan of expediency. Either way, I wasn't one to complain.

"That's it, baby," Shield praised as I crouched before him, swallowing his cock. "Breathe through your nose, Audrey."

I frowned, pulling away and ignoring his groan as he slipped from my mouth.

"Shield, I think you're labouring under a misconception as to what the human body is capable of." I pointed to my throat. "I can breathe through my nose until you reach the nasopharynx, then it is physically impossible for air to pass to the trachea. At that point, you're essentially strangling me with your penis."

His face took on a funny twist.

"Babe."

"Yes?" I asked, tilting my head to one side.

"Choking on my cock is not a turn-off."

My eyebrows rose. "Really? But what about the gagging sounds?"

"Suck my cock and see."

I sucked in another breath and pushed forward, determined to take him even deeper.

He groaned, the broken sound feeding my desire.

"Audrey."

He tasted of heat and salt and man.

Delicious.

I glance up to find him staring at me with those smouldering dark eyes.

I give him a tight suck, forcing him further into my throat.

"Fuck." Shield grunts, fisting my hair. "You little brat."

I hum around his cock, pleased to have startled him.

"You like sucking my cock, pretty girl? You like feeling me deep in your throat?"

And just like that, he turned the tables on me.

Desire pools deep in my belly, my response immediate. I've become Pavlov's dog, and his praise was my bell.

I renewed my efforts, desperate to taste him coming down my throat. But Shield had other ideas.

Hauling me off him, he ignored my protests to press me against the tiles, my legs automatically wrapping around his waist.

"Planned to do this in a bed," he muttered. "Can't wait." Reaching behind him for his jeans, he pulled a condom packet from a pocket and shifted slightly. Tearing the foil with his teeth, he rolled the condom down his cock—the action shockingly erotic.

Eager to have him in me, I shifted, wrapping my arms around his shoulders.

"Ready?" he asked, searching my face.

"You are cleared for launch," I whispered.

He stuttered out a laugh and pressed his cock to my entrance.

We both sobered, our desire peaking. Slowly, ever so slowly, he sank into me, his cock hard and thick.

My head tipped back, my eyes closing as he worked himself in.

Thick, hard, long. He really does have an exemplary penis.

And that was my final thought as Shield drew back only to thrust into me once more.

"Shield!"

He held me in place, pinned like a butterfly to a board as he fucked me over and over, his cock a terrible delight.

His mouth was everywhere, at my shoulder, my neck, my ear, catching my needy whimpers and issuing hot demands as he fucked me again and again, his thick cock stretching me to my limits.

The pleasure-pain reached fever pitch, and then he changed position—tossing me over the edge of my orgasm and into the most soul-wrenching climax of my life.

I screamed as he worked me, hitting every nerve ending and pleasure sensor in my body.

Distantly, I heard him come, his thrusts turning choppy.

Sucking in air, I groaned.

"Shit," he pulled me away from the shower tile. "Did I hurt you?"

I shook my head. "No, I'm just disappointed."

He blinked. "Sorry?"

I pouted as his cock slid from within me. "You came."

He blinked again.

"That means we can't go a round two."

"Audrey, babe," his voice sounded funny like he had a tickle in his throat. "We are doing round two. Not right now, but later today. When there's a bed. And a door. And we're alone."

I perked up. "Promise?"

He slid me down his body until my feet touched the ground. Holding me steady, he raised one hand, his pinkie held out to me.

"Pinkie swear."

I grinned, then hesitated. "Shield?"

"Right here, babe. "

"Later, I mean, if there is a later—"

He chuckled. "There will be."

"Oh, well... during that session, could you maybe talk dirty to me?"

He raised an eyebrow. "Am I not?"

"No, I mean...." I hesitated, unsure how to ask for what I wanted. "More? Like... dirtier?"

"Dirtier?" he asked, stepping into me. His hands settled on my hips, his palms warm and rough against my skin. "Like what?"

I shrugged, uncertain of how to verbalise what I wanted.

"You want me to call you a slut, baby girl? You want me to talk about how I'll use your sweet cunt and claim it?"

Goosebumps broke out over my skin, a pleasurable shiver snaking down my back. In silence, I nodded, staring up into his dark eyes.

A slow smile crept across his face.

"Alright, my naughty girl. I'll do it. Next time." He abruptly stepped back, leaving me feeling off-balance.

"Not now?" I asked, cringing at the whining tone of my question.

"No." He reached for a towel, briskly running it over his body. "We have things to do." He glanced at me. "Besides, I want you to beg for it the next time I take you. I want you so wet and wild, you'll let me use you however I want."

He turned his back on me. "Get dressed, babe. We have work to do."

Gulping, wet and more than a little turned on, I dressed, wondering what I'd signed myself up for.

15

AUDREY

Red, cloying dirt stretched out before us in a never-ending expanse. Seated on the passenger seat beside me, Killer panted quietly, her head tilted back to allow the wind whipping through the window to whip at her floppy ears.

I'd never grow tired of that hit of adorableness.

In the back seat, Zero and Lottie slept, leaning on each other, their soft snores playing background to the dull roar of the road.

I drove, relishing the white noise. It allowed me time to process the last few days and begin planning for the next stage of our slow movement north.

Shield led our small contingent on his motorcycle. I didn't envy him—the ride looked like a bumpy, dusty hell.

We'd delayed our departure by a few days to ensure Farmer was well on his way to full health. Despite his injuries, the guy held court from his bed, overseeing the repairs and refortification of the walls.

The next time someone approached his territory with

malicious intent, he and his people would make sure it would be the last bad decision they ever made.

We'd been travelling for three days, camping under the stars and cooking over open fires. My time with Shield had been limited to heated glances and the occasional conversation as he planned routes, checked vehicles and organised our security shifts.

Even out here in the middle of nowhere, danger lurked.

The red dust gradually gave way to scrub. The golden afternoon light danced through the trees as we transitioned from dirt roads under big open skies to gravel and, eventually, bitumen. Shield held up a hand, signalling a turnoff. Leading us away from the main highway and onto a gravel secondary road, we travelled for a time before the road spit us out at a campsite.

I parked the SUV, grinning as I took in our beautiful surroundings. Once upon a time, this would have been a teeming campground filled with families and grey nomads making their way across our sunburnt country. Now it had been reclaimed by nature, with high grasses and an abundance of insect life.

The dry red dirt contrasted sharply with the silvery-grey and green leaves of the native species, reminding me of the rugged uniqueness of this country.

There is beauty in the wild.

"We'll stop here for the night," Shield called, slapping dust from his clothes. "There's a gully down that way for water and washing. The composting toilets won't be much to write home about, but at least they're private." He glanced around. "Let's establish a perimeter and set up camp. I don't expect any company, but let's double-check."

The men spread out, setting up a perimeter along the tree line as the women took over refuelling duty. It may have seemed sexist, but the fact of the matter was these men were trained in combat—we weren't. And a few skirmishes and a little weapons instruction did not make us experts.

Refuelling took time—and was an essential job. We used one of the tankers in anticipation of discarding it should the need arise. Jo had modified the valves to allow us to drain small amounts of fuel from the storage tanks into jerry cans. Each of us would then haul the filled cans one at a time to the waiting bikes and vehicles.

"When we get to Cunnamulla, I'm going to rework this," Jo grumped, huffing as she dragged the can across the ground. "We need the option to hook the vehicles up to a hose and pump directly from the tanker."

I nodded, grimacing. "That would be useful. By the time we finish doing this, I'm too exhausted to do anything else."

Ellie groaned, pressing a hand to her lower back. "One more trip, and we should be done."

While we finished fuelling, Lottie and Zero had scoped out a place for our tents—stamping down the long grass and removing any lumps, clearing a space for our fire pit, and cutting a path from the tents to the toilets and down to the water.

Kate, meanwhile, was in a plant-life-induced state of ecstasy. After days of minimal foliage, the botanist was hunting through the camp, exclaiming over various seeds, wildflowers and succulents that grew through the area.

"You think we can eat any of that?" Ellie asked, nodding at Kate.

"I hope so." Jo swiped her arm across her head. "Hey, Kate. What have you found?"

Kate's head jerked up, her face a wreath of smiles. "Atriplex nummularia!" She brandished a handful of leaves triumphantly.

"In English?"

"Old Man Saltbush."

"Does it make alcohol?" Zero asked, stacking rocks around a small fire pit.

"Better! You can eat it."

"That doesn't sound better," Zero muttered, returning to the rocks.

My mouth watered. "What's it taste like?"

Kate tilted her head to one side. "The leaves taste salty. They're often wrapped around meat to marinate it, can be ground up for seasoning, or you can collect the seeds and add them to various foods for protein."

Kate bent again, plucking more leaves from the abundant plant. "Just wait until you try tonight's dinner. It's going to be next level."

With the perimeter secure, the other men returned, and the camp was quickly established. Bug spray was liberally applied as the sun began to sink low on the horizon, and Kate got to work building a fire to cook our dinner.

"Stew again," Jo sighed, taking a seat on a log next to the fire. "I'm so over stew."

I grinned. "You wouldn't if Yana was here."

Jo chuckled. "True. The woman has a way with food."

Our friends back in Adaminaby would be enjoying from her cooking. The chef had turned even the most basic of meals into a gourmet experience. She'd joined us because her sister, Aella, had stayed. A nursing student, Aella had been invaluable to us, and Yana had proved to be just as valuable, cheerfully taking over all cooking duties, supervising the maintenance of the kitchen garden, and demonstrating how to preserve the food we harvested.

Everyone pulled their weight in the After.

"Audrey?"

I glanced over my shoulder to find Shield holding two large water tanks.

"You want to come help me?"

For a split second, I considered refusing. I needed to put him back in his corner, keeping him at arm's length from my heart.

He was a good man, and I couldn't allow him to gain a foothold.

"Please?" he asked, wiggling one of the containers.

With a beleaguered sigh, I stood, dusting my pants off. "If I must."

He grinned. "I'll make it up to you."

I patted him on the chest, accepting one of the water tanks. "I expect nothing less."

He fell in beside me, our silence companionable as we moved away from the campsite. One might look at this arid land with its sunbathed land and red dirt and assume it was barren and unappealing. But the ruggedness and unapologetic wild called to me. Even here, life went on. Insects and tiny birds fluttered about, their noise a soothing balm to my aggravated soul.

"It's funny," I said, breaking our silence. "I've seen more of this country since the world ended than I ever did in the Before. Sure, it's necessary travel. But I wonder if I'd have done the same if the world hadn't ended." I spread my arms out to encompass the rugged terrain around us. "I'd have missed the beauty."

Shield walked on, seemingly content to listen to me.

"My parents moved to this country a few years before I was born. I've been to Vietnam several times with them, but it never felt like home." I touched a leaf from one of the trees as we descended into the gully.

"I've travelled—seen more of Australia than most

people, I suspect. Went overseas, too—both on duty and as a tourist. But no *where* feels like home to me." Shield jumped down from the path to a small rock shelf, holding a hand out to help me do the same. "Home isn't a place for me. It's the people I love."

"I like that idea, but I'm not sure it holds true for me."

"No?" Shield jumped down to another shelf, holding out his hand once again. "Why?"

"All my people are gone."

"What about your friends? What about the Club?"

I shrugged, handing him the water canister. "Maybe."

He dropped the canister beside him, holding a hand for me to take. I stumbled a little on landing, but Shield caught me, steadying me with a hand on my belly. I glanced up, finding his gaze dark and hungry.

"Oh," I murmured, realising why he'd asked me to accompany him. "You want sex."

He grinned. "Always. You up for it?"

I glanced around. "We're awfully open out here, aren't we?"

"Not for long. Follow me."

And like a lamb to the slaughter, I did just that.

16

SHIELD

I'd passed through this way multiple times over the years, always marvelling at the changing landscape.

Tucked away from the main campsite and some ways down the river sat a hidden oasis. Sand lined the bank on one side, river-softened rocks on the other. In the middle, a deep pool of clear water flowed lazily past.

Sheltered on either side by old gum trees and towering rocks, the cove provided the privacy needed to seduce my woman.

My woman? Since when did I start thinking of Audrey as mine?

Dropping the can to the sand, I began to strip, removing first my weapons, then my clothes.

"What is it with you and water?" Audrey asked, her hands going to her own clothes.

"You said you wanted me clean every time."

Her fingers stilled on her clothing, her eyes wide behind her glasses. I could see her processing something, the thought bubble practically hovering above her head.

I briefly considered forcing her to verbalise but left her to her thoughts.

She'd soon understand that I took my role in her life seriously—even if this was only meant to be temporary.

Naked, I gathered my clothes, tossed them into the river, and following them in.

"What are you doing?" Audrey yelped, making a move to try and catch them.

"Washing."

Dunking my dust-caked jeans into the water produced a plume of reddish water. I did the same with the rest of my gear, checking it for wear and tear. When clean, I tossed them onto one of the sun-warmed rocks to dry.

Audrey followed my lead, stealing glances at me as she did so.

"What?" I finally asked when she'd finished.

"I'd assumed you'd want to go to pound-town as soon as we were naked."

I blinked, then threw my head back, roaring with laughter.

"Babe," I shook my head. "Don't ever call it 'pound-town' again."

She grinned. "Why not? It made you laugh, didn't it?"

"Come here."

She swam over, and I folded her into my arms, supporting us both as we floated.

"The reason I didn't immediately jump you is because I want to take my time." I jerked my head to the sun sitting low on the horizon. "We got another hour, maybe two, before dark. The clothes can dry while I devour you."

Her eyes brightened. "And by devour, do you mean more oral?"

I chuckled, kicking once to push us toward the shore. "You seem to have a thing for my mouth, Ms. Audrey."

She sighed, her legs wrapping tighter around me. "Your mouth is nearly as good as my vibrator."

"Nearly?" I asked, swallowing more laughter.

"Well, it does take a little while to get me in the moment. With the rose, it'll tickle my clit from the start. I have masturbation down to five minutes."

I wrapped an arm around her back and another under her ass, hauling us from the water. She yelped, clutching at me as I strode across to the sandy area.

"Five minutes? That's not masturbation, that's a performative release."

I slid her down my body, holding her hips to keep her in place.

"Babe, self-pleasure—any pleasure—deserves to be savoured."

She blinked. "But who has time for that?"

I bent, catching her ear lobe between my teeth. I nipped gently, then sucked the sting away.

"You make time."

Her skin tasted of sunshine and the promise of summer. Kissing my way down her body, I nipped and sucked, detouring to areas hereto unexplored.

Her collarbone drew low moans, her breasts soft begging. The curve of her belly had her giggling, while nibbles along her hip bones had her fingers clenching in my hair.

"Shield."

I parted her thighs, crouching in the sand. Her sweet scent invited me, her fingers pressing into my head encouraging me to taste, to linger, to enjoy.

And enjoy I shall.

"You taste so fucking good, baby. So wet for me. You wanted this, didn't you? Your greedy cunt has been begging for me to taste you."

She stiffened then moaned, her pleasure at my filthy words obvious.

Someone likes being naughty.

I danced my tongue along her sensitive skin, amused by her whispered pleas. Concentrating my efforts on her clit, I circled and teased, committing her taste to memory, feasting upon her like a man starved of pleasure.

Audrey cried out, bucking against my mouth, her desire coating my face as she came. Her legs buckled and I shifted, laying back in the sand and guiding her down over me.

"Again," I ordered roughly, urging her to sit on my face. "Come here, baby. You're gonna come all over your President, aren't you?"

She licked her lips. "Yes."

"Say it."

"I'm going to come on my President."

"Now do it."

She shuffled up my body, positioning herself on my face. I wrapped one arm around her hips to hold her in place, my other hand working between us to play counter to the hot heat of my tongue. Audrey cried out as I parted her once more.

I pressed a finger to her entrance, gratified when she bucked, her hips lifted to grant me access. Her greedy pussy pulled at me, clutching desperately at my blunt finger as I fucked her roughly.

Brutal, raw, desperate. My woman released animalistic sounds as I forced her to come again and again on my face. My cock begged for attention, rigid and hard, but I ignored it, desperate for one more orgasm from her.

Her body arched, and again her legs squeezed my head as she cried out, coming in a lusty, beautiful mess.

"Shield," she gasped, clutching at my hair. "Please!"

With a grunt, I hauled her up, lifting her down my body to position her over my cock.

"Take it," I barked, pressing against her entrance. "Take me, my little cock slut."

She moaned, forcing herself down and onto my waiting dick.

Heat encompassed me, and a vague concern tickled the back of my mind. Lost to sensation, I fisted Audrey's hair, dragging her down to suck her cream from my tongue as I fucked into her tight cunt.

"Lick yourself from my face."

Her tongue darted out, licking across my lips, chasing her taste. Her pussy clenched around me, tight and wet, hot and desperate.

"You love this, don't you, Audrey? You love being forced to pleasure me. You want me to use you, sweetheart. You're begging me to treat you like a little cum slut."

She panted, nodding as I began to jack my hips, fucking her slow and deep.

"So tight, baby." I caught her whimpers with my mouth, grinding my dick into her. "So, fucking wet. You're such a good girl, aren't you? You're gonna pleasure your President, aren't you? Now be a good little cum slut and take my dick nice and deep. That's it. Lean back, baby. Cup your breasts and play with your pretty tits while I make you feel good."

She clenched around my cock, whimpers escaping her as she moved to do my bidding. Her hands cupped her small tits, her gaze locked with mine as she played with her nipples, stroking and circling, teasing herself as I enjoyed the show.

I pressed a hand to her belly, uncertain how she might take this but determined to test her boundaries.

"You want me to fill your tight snatch? You want me to mark you, Audrey?"

She groaned, her hips rocking against me.

"Say it."

"Yes."

I drew back, my hands clamping on her hips to hold her in place.

"You want me to breed you, baby? To fuck you until everyone knows who you belong to. Until you're round and full of my seed."

Audrey gasped, her gaze flashing.

"Oh, you want it, you fucking filthy girl."

I fucked up and into her, slamming my cock into her tight channel. This was no slow build, no gentle lovemaking. This was fucking—pure and brutal.

And Audrey got off on it.

She lit like a fucking firecracker, going wild. Her nails raked down my chest, her body bowing as she offered herself to me—a willing sacrifice to a conquering warrior.

"Take it," I ordered, fucking her. "Squeeze my cock, baby. Fuck my dick. Make me—"

She came with a strangled scream, her body bowing, her hips bucking as I hung for the ride.

Her tight snatch squeezed me like a fucking vice, rendering me powerless to stop my own orgasm.

Gasping, Audrey collapsed onto my chest, our bodies still locked together.

I could feel her gasping breaths against my skin, the sweat on her body cooling as we came back to Earth.

Finally, Audrey raised her head. "You came in me."

I winced. "Yeah. Sorry about that. Won't happen again."

She shook her head. "I took a contraceptive shot before leaving Adaminaby. We're fine for another few weeks. And I have a clear bill of health. " She bit her lip. "I liked it. I like...." She reached down to touch where we were still joined.

"Yeah?" I rolled until she was under me, the sand at her back. "I'm clear too. Last I checked and there's been no one since."

She blinked. "Does this mean we could...?"

I ground my groin against her. "You like this?"

She nodded, her gaze darkening. "Are you—"

"Hard again?" I grinned darkly. "It seems the idea of filling you with my cum provides me with an incentive to shorten my recovery time." I pressed my forehead to hers. "You're sure?"

She wrapped her legs around me, pulling at my hips with surprising strength.

"Definitely."

Hard again, I kissed her, vaguely surprised when she bit my lip.

"You little bitch," I chuckled, reaching out to straighten her glasses. "Now you're in for it."

Her lips parted, a smile lightening her face. "I certainly hope so."

Hours later, we returned to camp with mosquito-bitten asses.

She was more than worth it.

17

SHIELD

Rather than press on to Cunnamulla, I'd declared a rest day. My people were exhausted, I'd seen it during the previous night's dinner. They'd been through hell over the past few months, and this little oasis in the desert provided a safe and badly needed reprieve.

After dealing with vehicle checks, minor equipment repairs, and some washing, my people scattered, finding their own spaces and activities for the afternoon.

I hijacked Audrey, taking her back to our cove. I'd already taken her gorgeous body three times, but my hunger for her hadn't abated. I'd never felt this before. Not this intensity. Not this overwhelming need to mark and claim and protect.

Even now, relaxed and reclined against a tree, I watched Audrey with the intensity of a wolf stalking his prey. Her hair was down and damp, curling slightly thanks to the wet heat of the afternoon. She wore my shirt and nothing else, her bare legs curled in the wet sand of the river bank.

Her fingers swirled through the water absently as she stared off into the distance, lost in her thoughts.

Selfishly, I wanted her thoughts to centre on me. I wanted all her thoughts, all her dreams, all her desires.

I wanted to be her everything.

"What are you thinking?" I asked, breaking the quiet of the afternoon.

Her fingers stilled. The slow-moving current caught the ripples, pushing them downstream.

"The world's population used to be about eight billion people. Of that, just under half are female." She sent me a glance. "Traditionally patriarchal societies disproportionately discriminate against female-presenting babies, which can result in abortions or female infanticide and neonaticide."

"Neonaticide?" I asked, wondering where Audrey was going with this.

"Intentional murder of a child within twenty-four hours of their birth."

"Ah." I grimaced. "That's a word I could have done without knowing."

Audrey lifted one hand to brush a chunk of her straight black hair from her face. "If we assume that women make up a crude number of three-point-nine billion, then we can begin to estimate the impact of the virus on populations."

I cocked an eyebrow, fascinated by the way her mind worked. "Go on."

She reached down to run her finger through the sand of the river bank, drawing numbers as she started to calculate.

"If the virus has a survival rate of two percent, and we know that women, children and the elderly had an infectious rate of eighty-four percent then we can assume...."

She frowned, beginning to check her figures. "Let's estimate that two billion are young, and another one point five are old. Then we make some assumptions about gender norms and average life expectancies...." She began muttering to herself as her finger flicked through the sand, creating a complex set of calculations.

Her brain worked in wild and mysterious ways. Logic and ration clashed with passion and persistence to create a woman brimming with curiosity and conviction.

There was nothing I wished more than to map every shadowed corner of her mind, even as I claimed her body.

You're mine, Audrey. Even if you don't know it yet.

I'd begun to make peace with the idea of taking her as my old lady. Were we moving fast? Yes. Was she worth it? Fuck yes.

"Two point seven billion. Give or take."

"Dead?" I asked, watching her scrutinise her sums.

"No, remaining living." She nodded once. "Though that's rough figures. It doesn't take into account those with minimal life expectancy, those living through starvation, those who were killed during the riots and invasions, those who have died since—"

I leaned over, capturing her hand to stop her cascade of words. "What prompted this line of thinking?"

She glanced down at our intertwined fingers. I wondered what she thought of my tanned rough skin against her cool sun-kissed silk.

"You said you hoped your sister was still alive. That she'd found somewhere safe and was not just surviving, but thriving." Audrey glanced up, tears glittering on her lashes. "I wanted to give you hope. To give you a figure you could use as a point of hope when you thought of her."

I reached out to brush the tears from her eyes. "And you did that, so why are you crying?"

"When I add in the starvation and her being in an unfamiliar land and—"

I chuckled, pulling her into my chest and crushing her with my arms. "Audrey, darlin'. You think I don't know the odds are against her?" I brushed a kiss against her forehead. "It's not odds that give me hope. It's knowing my sister. It's knowing the strong, powerful woman she is. It's knowing she is resourceful and cunning. She's courageous and will do whatever she needs to survive."

I leaned back a fraction, looking down into Audrey's big, whiskey-coloured eyes. "There is next to no chance of meeting her again in this lifetime. Of hearing her voice or seeing her face. But in my heart, I can imagine a world in which she's happy. And someday we'll be reignited in whatever afterlife exists out there."

Audrey sniffled, her lower lip wobbling just a fraction. "I don't believe in the afterlife. Organised religion isn't something I subscribe to."

"No?" I dropped one hand to brush a finger against her nipple. "You sure about that? I could have sworn you were calling for God last night."

I heard her breath catch. Her gaze locked with mine as she leaned into my caress.

"Are you proposing to show me heaven?"

A grin stole across my face. "Baby, I thought you'd never ask."

I shifted her back a little in my lap, creating space to reach between us and free my cock from my boxer briefs.

I fisted my dick, using some precum to glide over my length.

"Do you like to watch, Audrey?"

I relished her shiver at my question, her dark gaze glued to my cock.

"Yes."

Her breathy confession caught me by surprise.

"Oh really?" I leaned back against the tree behind me, creating space to begin slowly stroking my dick. "Tell me more."

She caught a drop of precum on her finger. She raised her hand to her lips and rubbed my seed across them.

"You naughty slut."

She blushed but held my gaze boldly. "In the Before, I enjoyed watching porn."

"And what was your favourite?"

She swallowed. "It depended on my mood, but...." She hesitated.

Fuck.

I leaned forward, abandoning my cock to cup her face.

"Audrey, no judgement. You like something, you like it. I'll tell you if it ain't my thing. But that doesn't mean I don't want to hear about it. If it gets you wet and begging for my cock, I want to know. If it's within my power to give it to you, I will. Your desires, your fantasies, the things that get you wet and aching—you don't have to apologise for those."

"I like sensual porn. Where there's lots of touching and fingering before they start pounding."

I let go of her face to reach down and wrap a hand around my dick, leaning back once more.

"Go on."

She licked her lips. "Masturbation or lesbian or female-female-male is good for that. Though I don't think I'm bisexual. I just like watching."

The thought of Audrey with another woman shouldn't have made me twitchy, but it didn't.

"I don't mind entertaining that fantasy, babe. But just to be clear, I don't share."

Her eyes danced behind her glasses. "That's okay. I'm also not interested in sharing."

I relaxed, stroking my cock again. "Do you use toys or fingers when watching?"

"Fingers," Audrey admitted, her gaze dropping to my dick. "Though I often get distracted and end up finishing with my vibrator instead."

I glided my thumb over the crown of my cock, enjoying the way her gaze watched hungrily as if memorising how I liked it.

I pointed my dick towards her.

"Taste me."

Her eyelids fell to half-mast, and slowly she reached up to remove her glasses. I took them from her, folding the arms and placing them safely on a rock behind me.

Audrey tossed off her shirt, then shuffled down and bent, her tongue flicking out gently to lap at my cock.

"Fuck." My head fell back as my hips twitched, a near-overpowering need to fuck her mouth hitting me.

She tugged at my briefs, and I lifted, letting her pull them off before settling back in the sand. She tossed them away and was on me, her eager mouth sliding half-way down my cock.

This might be the best-worst idea I've ever had.

Audrey pulled back her tongue playing with my tip before she bent once more, her mouth hot and so fucking wet around me. I watched her take me as I rained filthy praise down on her.

"That's right, Audrey, you suck me deep. Good girl. Fuck, your mouth feels good, baby. You look so sweet with my cock buried between your lips. So, fucking sexy with that ass in the air. Yes, honey. Choke on me. Take my dick deeper, baby. Yes." I hissed, my head falling back. "Fuck."

Her hand came up, capturing mine. I thought she

wanted to hold on to me only to have her guide me to her hair.

The look in her eyes said it all.

"You're gonna watch, pretty girl. And you're gonna enjoy every fucking minute." Fisting her locks, I tugged her head back, gratified by her startled, sexy moan.

"You naughty fucking slut," I praised, leaning forward. "Are you trying to get me to fuck your tight cunt?"

She hesitated for a beat too long. "No."

"Liar." I dropped her hair and reached for her, hauling her up my body and holding her above me as I twisted her around until her back was against my front, my cock pressed against her ass. The move had her off-centre, her hands reaching out to steady herself before she settled back against me.

With her head tucked against my shoulder, I placed her hands on her breasts.

"Keep them here but play."

She shuddered against me but did as ordered.

Gripping her thighs, I roughly spread her legs. Holding them in place, I ground my dick into her ass, waiting for her to start squirming.

I ran my hands up her inner thighs, teasing as she played with her breasts, tugging at her nipples and rolling her thumbs over their erect peaks.

With a deliberate crudeness, I spread her with one hand, holding one of her thighs with the other.

"You see?" I whispered in her ear. "You're at my mercy now, Audrey. I could do anything I want to you."

Her breathing turned choppy, a flush colouring her inky skin.

"Thankfully, all I want to do is make you come."

I danced fingers across her clit, circling and stroking,

pressing and flicking, each sudden change carefully formu-
lated to keep her focus on me.

"Shield...." Her sweet moans sent what little blood
remained in my body straight into my dick.

I brushed my lips against the shell of her ear. "Tell me
what you want, Audrey."

Her hips flexed, her head turning as she stared up into
my eyes. Her gaze was unfocussed, clouded, but bright with
need.

"You. In me. Your cum—"

"Fuck."

I worked her over, pushing her, fingering her pretty clit
until she broke under my hand. Her body bowed, her
mouth opening on a scream I chose to swallow. Her lips
tasted of desperate hunger and grinding, hurting need.

"You want my cum?" I growled against her lips, my fingers
burying in her soaked pussy. "You want me to fill you up?"

"Yes!"

"Then ride me, baby. Take what you want."

She scrambled, twisting in my lap until her sweet cunt
lined up with my cock. Placing hands on my shoulders, she
adjusted, staring down at where our bodies would join.

In one agonising move, she slammed down, seating
herself on my dick.

FUCK.

I grunted, leaning forward to bite her shoulder. I needed
to mark her, brand her, claim her as mine.

There was no escaping Audrey. Not today. Not ever.

Mine.

"Good girl," I praised, my hands on her hips as I guided
her up and down my dick. "Fuck me. Take me, baby girl.
Ride my dick."

"Tight," she panted, her head falling back. "So big."

I chuckled darkly, barely holding on. "Finger your clit, Audrey. I need to feel you coming around me."

She slowly shook her head.

"No?" I raised one hand to grip her throat, applying the smallest amount of pressure. "You're refusing your President?"

Her breath caught, and I saw a flash of unexpected desire before she masked it.

She likes to be choked.

To test my theory, I tightened to squeeze, groaning when her pussy throbbed around me.

"You naughty girl." I pulled her towards me by her throat —gently and with care, but Audrey didn't seem to realise that. She whimpered, her hips picking up speed.

"You're mine, Audrey. I'm claiming you. Which means you answer to me. And if I say, play," I thrust into her roughly. "You do it."

Her hand dropped to thumb her clit, her eyes wide as she rubbed.

"Good girl."

I released my hold on her neck and nipped her instead, immediately sucking the sting away. I lingered, ensuring I left a mark to brand her as mine.

"You're gonna play with your pretty cunt until you come, Audrey. Then you'll fucking milk my cock, take my load, say thank you and ask for more. Got it?"

She nodded, now incapable of words, her body jerking with the motion of my thrusts.

"Good girl. Now." I wrapped my hand around her throat, this time cutting off her breathing. "Come for me."

Her pussy gripped me, her orgasm crashing into her.

Audrey bowed backward, her tits tilted to the sky as she came, shuddering and squirting over my cock.

"Fuck," I grunted, drawing out her orgasm, never wanting this to end.

She's mine. All mine.

"Shield," she gasped, under my hand. "I need—I need—"

"I know exactly what you need."

I dropped my hands to her hips, holding her in place as I fucked into her—hard, fast and brutal. I used her, giving my girl exactly what she wanted.

She exploded, screaming and clawing at me, her little teeth nipping at the skin of my neck while her sweet pussy squeezed my dick over and over until I came.

Roaring my release, I emptied myself into the woman who owned me—mind, body, and soul.

I collapsed against the tree, Audrey slumping onto my chest, my arms holding her close as we fought to catch our breath.

The sun dipped, the shadows growing longer until finally, Audrey raised her head.

"Do you think you can go again?" she asked, her gorgeous eyes staring into mine.

I huffed out a laugh. "Four times in one day, babe. You'd worn me out."

"So that's a no for number five?" she sounded disappointed.

"For me, yes. For you?" I pressed a hand to her pussy. "Never."

"Yay."

18

AUDREY

The SUV bounced over a large hole, rocking from side to side. I glanced in the rear vision mirror, grinning when Lottie and Zero blinked sleepily before settling back into each other.

There was a slow-burn romance I hadn't seen coming.

Unlike your own.

My thoughts turned away from our travel to the man in question. The sensible thing would be to cut him off. I'd gotten what I needed from him—a clearer mind. But a new addiction had taken root, one that begged for more kisses, more touches, more Shield.

It shouldn't have surprised me—the man had a body I found physically pleasing. But add in that he was nice, generous, and seemed to find me fascinating? Well, it was proving to be a disaster in the making.

No relationships.

I had to keep reminding myself that I was better off without people. I'd begun to get comfortable and complacent, relying on individuals and becoming more interconnected in their lives.

No more. It's time to put the boundaries back in place.

There were some relationships I'd be unable to unwind, like my friendship with Ellie—they'd existed long before the world had ended. They were the primary reason we'd been able to bring together the women in our lives.

But others could be removed or reshaped to become less emotional and more transactional.

Like Shield. Put him back in the physical release box. You let him slip. Don't allow it to happen again.

Decision made, I reached out to pat Killer.

"We have everything we need."

Are you sure?

I ignored the voice in my head.

In the dying hours of the day, we arrived at Cunnamulla. Driving through the barren town with its abandoned houses and cars after days of rugged beauty brought home the era of humanity in which we now lived.

This is either the start of the end or the beginning of something new.

Palm trees swayed in the hot spring wind while a mob of kangaroos, startled by the sound of our vehicles, hopped down the main street.

We followed Shield as he led us through the abandoned streets and out to the other side of the ghost town. Down a long road, we followed until he turned off and into a driveway. The dirt drive was long and winding, taking you through a brick fence and into dense scrub.

The land was flat, the red dirt peeking through the brush. Here and there were kangaroos or emus, each raising their head as we drove past.

"Where are we?" Lottie asked, leaning forward in her seat.

"The Bunker," Zero answered, tapping his hand against

the glass window. "It's the biggest piece of land we own. One of the brothers left it to us decades ago. It was a military base training base, then a cattle station. A farm another time. More recently, it was our Clubhouse—the half-way point for those who wanted a little peace and quiet."

"And now?" Lottie asked as we followed another twist in the long road.

"Now it's a sanctuary for the chapters in this region."

"Can anything survive out here?" I asked, grimacing at the dust cloud left by the vehicles in front of us.

"Yes, but not without help."

We followed the track another kilometre before a structure rose in the distance, shimmering on the horizon.

"Is that it?" Lottie asked, pointing at the tower.

"Yep," Zero confirmed. "That's the Bunker."

We drew closer, and I was surprised to see towers and walls made from rusted and beaten metal.

"Are we safe?"

Zero chuckled. "They make 'em different out this way. But yes. You're safe. You're Club."

Men and women lined the top of the giant wall, their guns pointed at us as we drew closer.

My hands tightened on the steering wheel, Killer growling low in her throat as she picked up on my tension.

"It's okay," I murmured. "We're okay."

Shield made a sign I didn't quite catch with his hands but the guns were lowered. A beat later, the giant fence slid open, granting us entrance.

We rolled through the gate and under a massive sign which read *Nameless Souls Motorcycle Club – Cunnamulla Chapter*.

A guy waved us through, pointing us to an area to park. My eyes widened at the reality of what we'd walked into.

"This is... wow."

At least thirty of Farmer's forts could fit in this dystopian castle. Housing, animals, market stalls and various workshops had been built to accommodate the needs of people. The original old Queenslander-style house sat in the middle, people bustling in and out as they went about their business.

I parked the SUV and climbed out, frowning as Shield climbed off his bike, shaking dust from his hair.

"I thought you said they were in desperate need."

"They are."

I gestured at the bustling settlement around us. "Sure doesn't look like it."

Shield frowned. "You haven't seen the stores."

"Thought we'd seen the back of you," a voice boomed across the courtyard.

Shield turned, grinning at the man walking toward him.

Tall and broad with dark skin and even darker hair touched with grey, his diamond earring glinted in the afternoon light. He reminded me of a pirate—debonaire with a roguish air about him.

"Never," Shield declared, slapping the stranger on the back. "You need all the help you can get."

Shield turned to me, placing a possessive hand on my lower back.

"Ash, meet Audrey, my woman."

I blanched, my head whipping to stare at Shield. "Your —what?"

"My woman." He stared down at me. "Right?"

Over his shoulder, I saw Kate making frantic cutting gestures under her throat.

"Um. Sure. I mean, yes."

Ash's eyebrow rose, but he kept his thoughts to himself

as he shook my hand. "Nice to meet you, Audrey. Welcome to the Bunker."

"Thank you."

"Ash is the VP here." Shield glanced over his shoulder. "Where's Rizzo?"

"The Prez is out on a hunt. But I'll send word. If you guys want to grab some chow and have a shower, our prospects can take you."

"Actually," Wrath interrupted, pulling Kate closer. "You got a blacksmith around here?"

Kate looked up at him, her eyes shining with unshed tears, her lips pressed together.

"A blacksmith?" I asked. "What's he need a blacksmith for?"

Jo shook her head, hushing me.

"Yeah, out back." The Vice President nodded at one of the prospects. "Take him to Smoke."

Wrath and Kate wandered off while Ash greeted the rest of our party and organised one of the prospects to lead us through the area on a quick tour. The size of the Bunker was impressive, and the walk through the various areas required the prospect to explain some of the rules and routines that were in place to make life easier for everyone.

"The old house is our headquarters. You need something, there are people in there who can point you in the right direction. Rizzo lives in the cottage out back. If you're okay with it, we'll put you up in the converted barn. We just finished turning the stalls into loft rooms. They're small but comfortable."

He pointed out new fortifications and discussed planned updates.

"And the stores?" Shield asked as our party drew close to the small cottage.

The prospect hesitated. "I'll let Rizzo and Ash explain. He should be back by now."

Sure enough, the VP and an older man were seated at a dining table, cool drinks accompanied by bread and fresh butter laid out before them.

The older man, Rizzo, had a shaved head, a close-cropped beard, and a swarth of tattoos up and down his arms.

We made small talk, eating our fill until Wrath and Kate reappeared, flushed and clean from a shower.

I shook my head, amused by their antics.

"It's bad," Rizzo said after they sat at the table. "We didn't get enough rain over the winter, and the crops aren't taking. The farmers are grumbling about a lean year, and the stores are already running low. We get more refugees heading this way every day." He sighed, pinching the bridge of his nose. "The meat is sustaining us for the moment—mostly kangaroos with the occasional pig or cow thrown in to keep morale up. But even that is a struggle."

"What do you need?" Wrath asked, pouring Kate a glass of water.

"A miracle." Ash laughed dryly. "Or rain. Anything that will get those crops to grow."

"M-maybe I can help," Kate offered. "I'm not a farmer, but I am a botanist and I've trained in horticulture. I understand how crops grow and what could be impacting them. I can advise on soil nutrients and which crops might be best placed where."

Rizzo's lift tipped up at the corners. "I'd be obliged if you could give it a go. Gods know that we've tried and failed. Even the old timers are struggling."

Ash ran a hand through his hair. "It's the soil. It's not the right consistency for crop farming." If we were about twenty klicks west of here, it'd be a different story."

"Then why not move? Or at least far in that area?" Ellie asked, reaching for another slice of bread.

"Bastards. The entire district is teeming with them. They arrived last autumn like a fucking wave of locus." Ash spat on the floor. "We survived by the skin of our teeth."

"And you're not afraid they'll come here?" Kate asked.

"There's a river between us and the bastards. It's keeping them on that side of town—at least for now. In the meantime, we need to farm. And until the bastards move on, we're stuck with the soil we have."

I tilted my head to one side, a shadow of an idea beginning to form.

The men caught up as the daylight faded. Food was served—roasted kangaroo and some vegetables. Lamps were lit, and outside, the bustling Bunker slowly turned quiet with the sounds of the night.

"I think we'll call it a night," Shield said, pushing back from the table. He stretched, his shirt riding up slightly on his stomach. "Thanks for dinner. We'll get Kate to check the fields tomorrow."

"The day after," Wrath corrected, his arm wrapped around Kate. "We're getting hitched tomorrow."

A beat of silence followed his declaration.

"I'm sorry," I said slowly. "Did you say... *married*? As in—" I made a circle with one hand, poking the ring finger of my other hand through it.

Kate nodded, a gorgeous smile lighting her face. "He asked, and I said yes."

"Holy shit. You're getting married." I pointed at Wrath. "And to *him*? You're sure?"

She giggled and pressed a hand to Wrath's stomach. "I'm sure."

"Well, shit. That's—"

"Oh my God!" Lottie screeched, throwing herself at Kate. "You're getting married!"

"I can't believe this," Ellie burst out, wrapping the two of them in a group hug. "How exciting! How can we help?"

"N-n-nothing to do. Just come and watch if you want."

"We want." Jo held her hand out for Wrath to shake, her gaze narrowing on him. "You better look after her."

"I will," he promised with an easy smile. "She deserves nothing but the best."

Unsure of how to compute this momentous event, I began to throw out facts and statistics about weddings.

"Did you know the earliest recorded wedding dates back to 2350 B.C. in Mesopotamia? And the word wedding is derived from the word wed, which means to pledge one's self? Brides used to wear—"

Kate pulled me into a hug, cutting off my diatribe.

"I know this is a massive change," she whispered, squeezing me tight. "But it's a good change. I promise."

I hugged her back, swallowing my question.

How can you be sure?

I LAY awake listening to Shield's even breaths beside me. We'd been shown to a set of converted apartments, the small spaces barely more than a cramped shower, toilet and bed. But it was warm, dry, and relatively quiet.

For the first time since I'd started sleeping with Shield, I'd begged off sex.

"I'm tired," I'd lied, turning away from him. "I'm sorry."

"It's okay, babe. No need to apologise. It's been a long few days." He'd kissed my shoulder and pulled me into him. "Sleep. Tomorrow will come soon enough."

Now here I was, hours later, staring at the moonlight as it slowly crept across the ceiling.

Married. A family. Maybe babies.

The thought terrified me. Kate had already lost so much —her mother, her friends, and now this? Wrath could be killed tomorrow, and Kate would be left with nothing but grief.

I closed my eyes, sucking another breath.

I didn't want to cut Shield out completely. But I also needed to shift us away from the intimacy he'd begun to build.

We can be fuck buddies. Nothing more.

Ways to achieve this fluttered through my head, one option after another, each considered and discarded until I found the perfect option.

A sex list.

I'd keep him so sexually busy that he'd have no chance to lure me in with deep conversations.

Because that has worked so well in every romantic comedy ever written.

I hushed the voice of doubt, satisfied that I knew exactly what I needed to do to keep Shield at arm's length.

You wish.

19

SHIELD

"Y ou made a list?"

Audrey held out the notepad. "You can see there's a rating scale. And room for us to include items such as angle, time to climax, and so forth."

Is this really happening?

An hour ago, I'd left Audrey sleeping in my bed. I'd washed, walked the permitter, and checked in with some brothers. I'd come back expecting to wake her with a slow morning session before we grabbed breakfast and walked across to the area Wrath had picked for this shotgun wedding.

Finding her awake and dressed, sitting cross-legged on my bed with reams of used paper around her as she frantically scribbled in a faded notebook, wasn't on my bingo list for today.

I took the offered pages and flicked through.

Sex positions.

Fantasies.

Desires.

The pages were filled—in alphabetical and numerical order—with everything Audrey wanted us to try.

"What prompted this?"

She shrugged, shifting from foot to foot. "You said I should ask for what I want." She gestured at the paper in my hands. "This is what I want."

"You actually want this?" I asked, tapping my finger against one entry.

She nodded earnestly. "I read that anal can be extremely pleasurable for a woman if done with a partner she trusts."

I cleared my throat. "You trust me?"

"Of course."

I cocked an eyebrow. "Babe, you barely know me. Giving your ass to someone isn't something you do on a first date."

She shrugged. "The data tells me you're a person of worth."

A person of worth?

"What the fuck does that mean?"

She raised her hand, ticking off her list on her fingers. "You're an elected leader who has managed to retain that leadership for a long period. You left the safety of your compound to travel to the other Chapters to ensure they're safe. You recognise when people are struggling and try to make their life easier. You thank people, no matter how small the gesture. You aren't above grunt work. You listen—actually listen—when people speak. You wait to eat until everyone else is served. You—"

She paused, blinking as if realising something.

"Oh," she murmured. "I *trust* you."

I tossed her notebook on the table, ignoring her yelp when I fisted my hands in her hair, closing the space between us.

"Audrey?"

"Yes?" she asked breathlessly, colour flushing her cheeks.

"Let's try number thirty-six."

Her eyes widened. "Really? But what about the wedding?"

Fuck.

I sighed, dropping to press my forehead against hers. "Fine. We'll go to the wedding. But after, we're doing number thirty-six."

She grinned. "Okay." Pulling away, she pushed at my chest. "Now go. I need to get ready."

"But—"

"Go!" She shoved me out of the door of our room and shut it.

I blinked, confused as fuck by what just happened.

"You know she's freaking out, right?" Pope asked from across the breezeway.

I frowned. "What?"

"Audrey. She's freaking out. She's convinced she doesn't do relationships. And I can almost guarantee seeing Kate and Wrath tie the knot today will hit her. Hard."

Pope pushed away from the wall. "You know she lost everyone when the virus hit. I heard it from Ellie—she was meant to be home that weekend but got tied up with some shit at the Uni. It's the only reason she's alive now."

I crossed my arms. "And you know this why?"

Pope shrugged. "She reminds me of someone." He glanced away, rubbing his chest.

His sister.

I didn't press further. "You think she's got survivor's guilt."

"Haven't we all?"

I sighed. "Sure. But some of us cope with it better than others."

"Now you got it, big fella." He stuffed his hands in his pockets, turning to walk away. "You got your work cut out for you, Prez. Hope she's worth it."

I watched him walk away.

"She is."

THE WEDDING TOOK place under a gum tree in the main yard. It was presided over by a blacksmith and witnessed by any who paused long enough to watch.

The bride wore a white gown and a crown of wildflowers. The groom wore his jeans, a clean shirt and his kutte.

There were no pictures, but I ensured the food flowed freely and drinking began at noon sharp. Within hours the revelry had turned into an all-out party. The bride and groom were sent to their 'honeymoon suite' while the residents of the Bunker partied long into the dark night.

I caught Audrey in a spin, pulling her into me as the music from the makeshift band shifted, slowing.

"Come," I whispered in her ear. "Follow me."

"Where?" she asked, allowing me to tug her away.

"You'll see."

We kept to the shadows until I came to the quiet corner I'd scoped out earlier that morning.

I pressed her into the back of the wooden barn, kissing her senseless.

I dragged my hands slowly up her body to cover her perky breasts.

"These have been driving me wild all night," I admitted. "Where'd you find this fucking dress?"

"Kate brought it with her."

I pinched her nipples through the thin fabric, grinning at her gasp.

"What are you doing?" she asked breathlessly.

"Giving you number thirty-six."

I abandoned her mouth for her neck, kissing and sucking my way down her sensitive skin.

"Shield, please."

I dropped my hands to her skirt, peeling the material up her legs to bunch at her waist.

"Hold this," I ordered.

She clutched the fabric. Her eyes were wide behind her glasses as I hooked my fingers into her underwear and peeled them down her long legs.

"Step out, baby."

She did so, using my shoulders as an anchor to balance.

"Good girl." I pressed her underwear to her lips. "Now open wide."

She hesitated a beat, then accepted the material, allowing me to stuff it in her mouth.

"Turned around, baby. Let me see your ass."

Her fantasy had asked for sex outside. This scenario was all for me.

"Bend," I ordered, running my hands up her legs and over the curve of her ass. "Place your hands against the barn.

She did so, and I grinned.

"Good girl."

I took off my belt, letting her hear the metal jangle.

"Now I'm going to fuck your tight cunt, Audrey. And you're gonna take it, aren't you?"

She nodded vigorously.

"Good girl."

I ran a hand down her ass and down to part her.

"Fuck, you're drenched." I guided my cock to her entrance, lining myself up. "You want this, don't you, baby?"

She nodded again, wiggling her hips and ass.

"Good." With one brutal thrust, I seated myself in her tight cunt, ignoring her gasping scream muffled by her underwear.

I held on to her hips, keeping her in place. "Fuck you're tight. Clench for me, babe. Force me to take you."

Her muscles tightened around my dick, and I groaned, fucking into her with a deliberate motion meant to hit her G-spot.

She reared back, her hands hitting the barn as her legs quaked.

Not long, not long, not long.

One stroke, two, three, and then she was exploding around me, her body a trembling, fumbling mess.

I caught her up, holding her to me as I came, filling her sweet cunt.

Gently, I pulled down her dress and removed the underwear from her mouth, tucking it in my jeans pocket.

"You okay?" I asked, holding her tight.

She nodded, her face pressed to my shirt.

I ran a hand over her hair. "You sure?"

She nodded again, then shook her head. Tilting her head back, she looked up at me with a strange expression.

"Shield?"

"Yeah, Babe."

"I think we need to break up."

20

———

AUDREY

It had been a week. A week of sleeping alone and avoiding the sexy, glowering, angry man who seemed to be everywhere I was.

I ate breakfast and he was there. I did laundry and he was there. I helped Kate in the field and—yep, you guessed it, he was there.

Every single time he asked the same question.

"Will you get back in my bed, Audrey?"

And every single time I answered the same.

"No."

My heart hurt. I missed Shield. I missed seeing him and tasting him. Talking and laughing with him. I missed the way he understood me when everyone else felt so out of step.

"You're moping," Ellie said, holding her hand out for a screwdriver.

I handed it to her with a heavy sigh. "I'm not moping. I'm just... missing good dick."

She snorted, twisting the screw into place. "You're missing more than that." She glanced at me. "You like him."

I grimaced. "Only in a professional sex sense."

"No, you like him as a man. And a friend. And a lover. And a potential partner." She pointed the screwdriver at me, giving it a small wiggle. "It's okay to admit you like him. I'm not going to judge."

I made a face. "It's not like that."

"No? Then tell me what it is like."

How does one describe having everything they desire in their hands but being too terrified of losing it to take a chance?

I shook my head. "It was just sex."

Ellie hummed under her breath.

"What?"

She shook her head. "For someone so smart, you're an idiot."

"Excuse me?"

She sighed, tossing the screwdriver onto the table beside me.

"You've never been the same since Jen died."

I stiffened. Jen had been our friend. She'd brought us all together. A college student, she'd been the life of the party, introducing herself and accepting me without judgement. It was through her that I met Jules, Lilith and Ellie.

Then she'd died. Just weeks before the pandemic. Young and in her prime, her life stolen by cancer.

"And then you lost your family. You used to be Audrey—open heart, open mind, loves everyone. You brought us together. You formed this band of sisters, yet you're trying desperately to push us away." Ellie crossed her arms over her chest. "I've been your friend for half a decade, Audrey. You and I both know how much Jen meant to us. And I get you lost your family—we've all lost people we care about. And after all that, Lilith and Jules go missing?" She shook her head. "It's fucked. This world is fucked. But closing yourself off isn't the answer."

My chest contracted my gut clenching.

Jen.

Sophie.

Mumma.

Dad.

Baba.

Papa.

John.

Jules.

Lilith.

These were the people in my life I'd lost. And each one had taken a part of my heart with them.

"You have Blair," I said, referring to her sister back at Adaminaby. "I don't have—there's no one left."

"Yes, there is!" Ellie thumped her chest. "There's me. There's Kate. There's Jo and Lottie and Pope. And you can bet your bottom dollar there's the man you've been fucking. What would you classify us as if not your people? Chopped liver?" She tutted. "Babe, you can't go around acting as if closing your heart off is the answer. Love and grief don't work like that. All it will bring you is regret."

I stared down at my feet, processing.

I already have regrets. So many I could fill the ocean with them.

With a sigh, Ellie pulled me into her arms. "Look, I'm not trying to bully you one way or the other. If Shield isn't the one for you, then that's fine. But the man looks at you like you hung the moon. And you, my darling, do the same to him. It's sickly sweet but also sexy as all hell."

I held on to her, needing the touch of another to admit what was in my heart.

"I'm scared."

She laughed. "Aren't we all?"

Ellie drew back, wiping at a tear I hadn't realised I'd shed. "But you're the bravest of us, Audrey. When all hope was gone, you came up with a plan. You did what had to be done. You forced us to survive. You made us who we are and brought our sisterhood together. We owe our lives to you. And I know that can never bring your family back—but we love you. And you deserve happiness."

I shook my head.

"Just think about it, okay?" She picked up the screwdriver. "Now, where were we?"

"Sorry to interrupt," Jo said, knocking on the door to the lab. "But I thought you might wanna know that a certain Major and her shadow just rolled up the driveway."

My heart froze in my chest. "Ava?"

Jo nodded, her grin wide. "And, not to get anyone's hopes up, but they have vehicles with them."

Jules and Lilith?

I turned on my heel and sprinted outside, my lungs heavy, my stomach churning.

Let them be alive. Let them be alive. Please, whichever benevolent being is out there, let them be alive.

I rounded the corner of the laboratory and spotted Ava. Joy bloomed in my chest, shocking but welcome.

"You're back!" I screamed, rushing across the yard. "Did you find them?" I demanded, throwing myself at Ava and wrapping her in a tight hug.

"Yeah, babe. They're in the car behind us."

I jumped back, staring at the truck that bumped along the drive, unable to believe my eyes.

Lilith sat in the driver's seat, Jules in the passenger. Both waved frantically at me, their smiles as big as my own.

"I knew you'd do it," I said, surprising myself with the conviction in my tone.

I'd not wanted to admit it, but I'd hoped beyond hope that she would succeed. I'd tempered my emotions, lying to myself about how invested I was in this outcome.

More fool you.

Ava sucked in a breath. "Well, shit. You could have told me that before I left."

I laughed. "I have so much to tell you. Kate and Wrath are married—"

"Wow," she said, blinking. "That's—"

"—and I had sex with a man," I rambled on, overcome with joy that she was here. "He's hot too."

"Pope finally pulled his finger out then?" Ava grinned, crossing her arms over her chest.

Pope? What is it with everyone thinking I'd sleep with Pope?

I wrinkled my nose. "Oh no, Pope and I are just friends. I could never have sex with a friend."

Her eyebrows shot up. "I'm sorry. What?"

"And my dog is pregnant," I sighed. "Lottie confirmed it yesterday. Do you guys want something to eat? We have—"

"Wait, Audrey." Ava held up a hand. "You had sex with someone who *isn't* Pope?"

I nodded vigorously. "Yeah, is that a problem?"

"I mean...." She glanced at Ghost, who looked bored out of his brain with this conversation. I didn't blame him.

"No?" she said finally, sounding uncertain.

"He's nice," I said, picturing Shield. "But bossy. I like it in the bedroom, but in real life it's just annoying, so we're on a break. He keeps telling me we're not, but we are."

The SUV pulled to a stop, Lilith and Jules tossing open the doors. Skirting Ava, I bolted towards them, wrapping the women in a tight hug.

"I missed you." I clung to my friends.

"We missed you too," Lilith said, her English Nigerian accent thick with emotion. "We have so much to tell you, Audrey."

"Are you safe?" I asked, stepping back to assess them with a critical eye. "Are you well?"

Six foot two with a flawless umber complexion and golden eyes, with a long, lean body, Lilith looked more like a supermodel than an electrical engineer. She was beautiful even with her skin dry and chapped in places, and her hair in a frazzled mess.

"We're good." Jules hauled me back in for a hug. "Fuck, I've missed your face."

Jules could not have been more different from Lilith. Short and plump with red-orange hair that tended towards frizz and a riot of freckles across her pale skin—she currently looked like a sunburnt Oompa Loompa, her tired eyes bloodshot and rimmed with dark smudges.

Kate, Jo and Ellie joined our welcome party with hugs, tears and news.

"Well, well, well," Pope called, strolling across the yard, his arms stretched wide in welcome. "If it isn't the prodigal son and daughter, returned to our welcoming bosom."

Beside me, Jules tensed.

"Hey." I glanced her way. "You okay?"

She nodded slowly, her gaze locked on Pope.

Behind him trailed the rest of the Adaminaby crew, including Runner, Butcher, Wrath, Texas, Swift and the now one-armed Zero.

"Where's Lottie?" Ava asked as the initial excitement settled.

"In theatre. One of the guys had a run-in with a snake.

They're everywhere around here, they tell me—" Pope broke off, stiffening as he caught sight of Jules. "Oh, fuck."

I glanced from Jules to Pope and back again.

"It's you," Jules said, her eyes wide.

"Wait, you know each other?" I asked, trying to keep up with this conversation.

"No," Jules denied.

"Yes," Pope answered.

"That is—" Jules started.

"We don't really—" Pope corrected.

They both fell silent, glaring at each other.

Amused, I tilted my head to one side. "Is this a sex thing?"

Jules, already beet-red from her sunburn, flushed magenta. "No, it's not a sex thing!"

Pope cocked an eyebrow. "You sure about that, Little Red?"

LITTLE RED?

Jules spluttered then turned on her heel, stalking away from us.

"Look," Ava said, interrupting this amusing interlude. "Can someone take me to my—"

Across the yard, Lottie screamed, running toward her sister. Ava took off, meeting her half-way.

Watching them, seeing their joy at being reunited—it hurt. I delighted in their reunion even as I knew the pain the uncertainty had brought.

Is loving worth the pain? How do you decide?

I saw Shield heading Ghost's way, his hands tucked into his pockets as he surveyed the scene.

My heart leapt, my stomach fluttering.

I love him.

I sucked in a breath.

Shit. I love him.

I watched him greet Ava and Ghost, his gaze searching the courtyard. Our eyes met across the space.

I love him. And I don't want to.

I pulled away from our small group, drawn like a moth to the flame.

"Ava, have you met Shield?" I asked, keeping my tone light.

She nodded.

I gestured at Shield. "He's the guy who fucked me."

Ava's head whipped from me to Shield and back. "*Him*?"

Shield glanced away, a muscle jumping in his jaw. I waited for him to meet my gaze, annoyed when he didn't.

Fine. You don't want to look at me? I'll make you.

I nodded, crossing my arms. "It was good. Not *great*. But good."

Shield startled, his gaze snapping to mine.

Game on.

"Babe," he said with a sigh, pinching the bridge of his nose. "I already told you, five is unrealistic. Not with the amount of shit I have to do every fucking day."

I rolled my eyes. "Kate said she and Wrath went five times without breaks."

"Is there a room for us around here?" Ava asked, her voice strained.

"We set you up in the old barn. They've converted it into rooms. You're number four. Do you want me to show you—?"

"I got it," Ghost rumbled, interrupting me.

He stared at Ava like she was his last meal.

Ah. I see they've consummated their arrangement.

"Oh," I said, nodding. "I see. You want to fuck."

Unable to stop myself from teasing Shield some more, I decided to offer some pointers.

"Ensure you do plenty of foreplay or try lube. I hear that helps." Shield's gaze darkened, his eyes flashing with heat. "Not that I've needed it," I said with a shrug. "But some people do. There should be some in each bedroom—I made sure when we moved in."

"Thanks, Audrey," Ava said, sighing a little.

"Anytime," I responded, turning away from Shield. "I'm quite good at giving sexual advice. Aren't I, *Lottie*?"

Shield's jaw clenched, and I delighted in seeing the flush creeping up his neck.

"Yeah, babe," Lottie answered, her voice strained.

Ava said something I missed but a moment later Ghost tossed her over his shoulder. I stared, open-mouthed as he carried her towards the barn, ignoring her protests.

"Oh," I murmured, watching them go. "That should definitely go on the fantasy list."

Shield stepped closer to me, his voice low as he dipped, pressing his lips to my ear.

"When you're ready to admit you want me, just say the words, Audrey."

I turned, ready to answer but he'd already slipped away.

Audrey – 0

Shield – 1

Full of confused angst, I did the only thing I could think of to distract me from my cyclonic thoughts—I hunted Pope down to demand the truth about him and Jules.

"Wait," I said, holding a hand up to Pope. "So, you're telling me that your sister is Jen. *My* Jen?"

He ran a polishing rag over the leather seat of his bike and sighed. "It appears so."

"But you weren't at her funeral."

His face shadowed. "I wasn't allowed."

I absorbed this, noting his closed-off expression.

Fisted hand, tense shoulders—he's deeply unhappy.

"Fine," I said with a dismissive flick of my wrist. "Then how did you not connect the dots before now? How many women named Jules, do you think attended St. Mary Women's College?"

Pope's jaw clenched. "Not enough, apparently."

I sighed heavily. "For someone with a decent intellect, you're rather obtuse sometimes."

His eyebrows rose, his lips tilting up at one side. "You don't say? In my defence, there was the whole ending of the world thing to consider."

"Not a reasonable defence. The world has been over for years." I patted him on the arm, feeling sorry for the doofus. "You're lucky you have me around. In addition to being of *superior* intellect, I am renowned for my observation skills and practicality."

I heard someone snort behind me.

"Audrey?"

"Yes?" I asked sweetly.

Pope's lips quirked. "Always change."

"I will."

He tilted his head to one side. "Now you've finished grilling me. Is it your turn?"

I crossed my arms, hugging myself. "There's nothing to grill."

"No?" He tossed the rag in a bucket and reached for a tool I'd never seen in my life. "You sure about that?"

I bit the inside of my cheek. "I don't want to have sex with Shield anymore. It's that simple."

The lie slid uneasily off my tongue, sounding strange

and uncertain.

Pope chuckled. "You're a crack-up." He glanced at me. "Babe, you're into the guy so deep you don't know you've already drowned. Why fight it? Why force yourself to deny what the rest of us already know?"

"And that is?"

"That he's into you, you're into him, and you two deserve to find a little happiness in this godforsaken world."

I'm hearing this a lot today.

I shook my head. "I'm good."

"Are you?" He turned back to the bike. "Cause you'd be the only one. The rest of us are damaged goods. Shield included. The guy lost his sister. Half his Club died. He's fought tooth and nail to keep us together, and then he finds a woman like you?" He waved a hand in my direction. "That's fucked."

I sucked in a breath. "What do you mean a woman like me? How is that fucked?"

Pope snorted, dropping one tool to pick up another. "Babe, you're awesome. You're hot. And let's be honest, you're likely the smartest person left on this planet. The guy is head over heels for you. And you just take that away?" He shook his head, screwing something onto his bike. "It's cold."

My heart seized. "It's not like that."

"No?" He dropped the tools, turning to face me. "Then what's it like?"

"It was just sex."

Pope's smile held far too much sympathy. "You want to try again?"

"It was—is—it—he—" I stopped, unable to process.

"Look, I get this is hard for you and you've been through a lot, and you've loved, and lost, and yadda yadda yadda." He waved a hand dismissively. "But so have the rest of us. I wouldn't have picked you for a coward."

"I'm not."

"No?" He turned back to his bike. "Then why are you running scared?"

"I'm not."

"You keep telling yourself that."

Dismissed, I exited the garage on numb feet, a million thoughts spinning through my head so quickly I could hold none.

The sun shone brightly, the sky a rich, clear blue. Under my feet, the red dirt was pitted with tiny wildflowers growing from cracks in the soil.

I closed my eyes, sucking in the rich, earthy smell of the land on which I stood.

You're alive. Why aren't you living?

Guilt. Grief. Anger. The words were too simple for the cauldron of emotions that swirled within me.

I didn't cause their deaths, but I didn't help them either.

Logically, I knew there was nothing I could have done. I'd been trapped in another state thousands of kilometres away. But guilt didn't work like that. Grief didn't understand reason.

I opened my eyes, staring out at the horizon.

I'm sorry.

I licked my lips.

"I'm sorry."

Tears burned the back of my eyes—tears I'd refused to shed.

"I'm sorry I wasn't there. And I'm sorry I lived when you died." A sob shuddered out of me, my shoulders shaking. "But Ellie and Pope are right. I deserve happiness. We all do."

I brushed at the tears now flowing down my cheeks. "I'll miss you. I'll always miss you. But I have to let you go. I can't keep you tied to this world."

Closing my eyes, I let the tears come.

"I love you all. See you in the next life."

My walls broke. A wave of emotions swept over me, crushing me under its weight. Sobs ripped from my chest, deep and guttural, raw with unexpressed grief.

A sound unlike any I'd ever heard exploded from my chest, ripping up my throat and out of my mouth—the call of a broken animal.

Strong arms wrapped around me, hauling me against a broad, warm chest.

"I have you."

Shield.

I tried to look up at him, tried to catch my breath to explain—but the tears wouldn't stop.

"Let it out, baby." Shield bent,' catching me under my knees to lift me into his arms, holding me tight against his chest. "You're safe, Audrey. I promise."

He carried me across the yard to the converted barn. Kicking the door to my small room open, he sat on the bed, still cradling me in his arms.

"That's it, good girl. Let it all out."

He gently removed my glasses and produced a handkerchief from somewhere, using it to capture my tears.

"I-I-I—" I tried to explain, to justify my hysterical state.

"Babe." He captured my head in his hands, brushing away my hair and staring at me with an understanding smile. "You don't have to explain."

"I said goodbye," I hiccupped, determined to get through this. "T-t-to my family. I haven't—when they died—I didn't cry. I couldn't. But n-now—"

He ran a hand over my hair. "This is good, baby. I'm glad you're processing." He pulled me back into his chest, holding me close.

"Let it out. I have you, Audrey. Promise."

All the horror and fear, grief and anger drained from me in an avalanche of tears. Finally spent, I slumped against Shield, too emotionally and physically drained to move.

He rubbed my back in slow, calming circles.

"Sleep, baby. You're safe in my arms."

With a sigh, I closed my eyes, welcoming sleep.

21

SHIELD

udrey woke hours later, frowning as she blinked at me.

"Shield?"

From my spot on the bed beside her, I ran a hand down her side, soothing her. "Right here, honey."

She blinked again, and I could see the fog clearing.

"Oh!" She jerked up into a seat, her hand going to her face. "Where are my glasses?"

I reached across to her side table and handed them to her. She shoved them on, blinking rapidly before her gaze met mine.

"You stayed."

My lips quirked. "Of course I did. I promised you'd be safe."

She swallowed, seemingly at a loss for words.

"Audrey, just because you don't want my body doesn't mean you don't have my heart."

Shit. Did I really say that?

I tested the truth of my words.

Well fuck. I guess we're admitting our feelings.

I cupped her cheek. "I love you, Audrey. There're no strings attached to this declaration. I'm not expecting anything from you."

"I'm not—that is..." she cast around, searching for her words. "I'm not an idiot."

I chuckled. "I never doubted that."

"Don't laugh, it's—" she struggled, her eyes welling with tears.

"Fuck." I fisted the back of her neck, pulling her into my chest to crush her against me. "Don't cry, baby. I'm not worth your tears."

"But you are!" Her voice was muffled against my chest. "*I'm* not."

"Bullshit."

She tipped her head back, her face damp. "I'm not! I can't communicate. I have no tact. I'm clever, sure. But I'm not the kind of woman you want standing beside you. I'll say the wrong thing, do the wrong thing. I'll ruin—"

"My whole life if you let those doubts win." I leaned back, staring down at her. "You're fucking perfect. I don't need bullshit facades. I don't need masks and smiles and people never telling you what they actually mean. I get enough of that—I've had a lifetime of it. What I want is you. I want your lack of filter. I want your brilliance. I want your sexy data testing. I want *you*."

She sniffled, her chin wobbling as she stared up at me, her big eyes full of tears behind her glasses.

"Are you sure?"

I grinned. "Pretty fucking positive."

I watched her process my answer—could practically see the cogs in her mind turning.

I hated that I couldn't protect her from the doubts that

assailed her. Hated that she was struggling with guilt and regret.

My whole life had been spent protecting the ones I loved from external dangers—but I had no power to combat the internal ones. I could only hope that I would prove to be the person who could help her silence the voices in her head.

"You love me?" she whispered, her gaze searching mine.

"More than I thought possible."

Her hand snaked up my chest to wrap around the back of my neck.

"Shield...."

I saw her big eyes well, heard the sharp intake of her breath.

"I love you too."

"Thank fuck." I caught her mouth in a hungry kiss. "Wait." I drew back, cocking an eyebrow. "Are *you* sure?"

I'd never seen a more beautiful sight than her smile.

"More than I thought possible," she echoed.

Unable to hold back my overwhelming need to claim her, I ripped off my shirt, tossing it away.

"Get naked. Now."

Audrey's mouth fell slightly open, her lips already swollen from my brutal kiss.

"But—"

"I need to claim you, babe." I fisted her hair, holding her steady. "And be warned—I'm not going to be gentle."

A little whimper slipped from between her lips, her eyes drifting closed. "Yes, please."

I ripped my remaining clothes off, tossing them about with abandon, pleased to see Audrey in just as much of a hurry.

Finally naked, I rolled to cover her with my body. Our mouths danced together, tongues twisting and stroking as we breathed each other in, hungry and full of desperate desire.

"You ready for me, pretty girl?"

Her hungry whimpers were a response I was powerless to deny.

Fisting my cock, I teased her with it, rolling my head around her clit.

"Fuck me already!" Audrey cried, her hips thrashing on the bed. "Shield, I need—"

I fucked into her, seating myself deep. We groaned in unison at my delicious intrusion.

"You're so tight, Audrey. Such a hot and greedy cunt. You want this, don't you, baby? You want me fucking you, marking you, filling you with my cum."

She went wild under me, her nails raking down my back, her teeth sinking into the flesh around my nipple.

"You fucking, bitch," I praised, holding her down as I pounded into her tight body. "You naughty, fucking girl. I'm gonna claim you, baby. Gonna make sure you know exactly who owns this pussy."

"You do," she said, staring up at me.

"And who am I?" I grunted, jerking my hips in time to my words.

"Shield."

"Again."

"Shield."

"Again."

"Shi—" Her orgasm ripped through her, gripping my cock in the tightest clutch I'd ever experienced.

Fuck!

I pulled back a fraction, looping one arm under her right leg, then the left, pushing them both up and to the side as I continued to fuck her sweet cunt.

The new angle pushed her over again, her scream ripping through the barn.

"Good girl," I barked, bending to bite her shoulder. "Let them hear you scream, Audrey. Let them hear me claiming you. I own you, baby. I own every fucking part of you."

"Shield!" She came again on a strangled scream, her head tossed back, her hands raking scratches down my back.

Magnificent.

I grunted her name, emptying myself in the woman I loved.

Spent, I collapsed next to her, both of us panting silently.

"Wow," Audrey murmured a moment later. "I don't remember putting that position on the list."

Raising my head, I stared at her for a beat.

"That's all you can say?"

She rolled onto her side, propping her hand under her cheek. Her eyes danced behind her askew glasses.

"Do you think we can make five this time?"

Laughing, I hauled her into my arms, delighting at her squeal.

"We can try."

EPILOGUE

Shield

"**W**here the *fuck* is my woman!?" I bellowed. The bustling yard froze as every head turned toward me.

I could feel the fear oozing from every pore in my body. Audrey and I had fought last night about something so inconsequential I couldn't remember what it was. But I'd woken to an empty bed. It was now hours later, the sun nearing its zenith, and I hadn't seen hide or hair of my woman.

And neither, it turned out, had anyone else.

Jules tripped across the yard, coming at a run.

"Ava says she won't have left the Bunker. She's too smart to put herself or others at risk."

My fear lessened knowing this was true.

"Then where the fuck is she?"

Jules grimaced, opening her mouth only for Pope to intercede.

"Hey, Prez, take a deep fucking breath," he snapped,

crossing his arms over his chest and planting his legs. "Jules is only trying to help. Stop taking your fear out on her."

I ran a shaking hand through my hair. "Shit, sorry. It's just—" I shook my head. "Fuck."

"It's okay," Jules said, laying a hand on my arm. "We'll find her."

Jo walked out of the garage, wiping her hands on a rag. Her hair stuck up at odd ends, grease and muck coating her dungarees and swiped across her cheek.

"Who are you looking for?" she asked, leaning against the barn door.

"Audrey. You seen her?"

She raised an eyebrow. "All this fuss for the genius?" She jerked her head toward the far tower. "She's up there. Has been since before dawn. Woke me up to help her haul shit up about a bazillion stairs."

I took off, pounding across the dirt. It may have made me look like a maniac, but I knew doubts still plagued her. She was getting better, moving past her fears and guilt and settling into the notion that she deserved happiness.

But there were still days where she struggled. And I refused to allow her even an hour of that struggle if I could help it.

Climbing the stairs two at a time, I burst through the tower door, skidding to a halt.

Standing in the centre of the tower, dressed in jeans and a black top, was my woman—proudly wearing a kutte that declared her as my property.

"—and he's great in bed," Audrey said into a mobile phone that was plugged into something that looked like a giant radio. "Talks really dirty." She grinned at me, beckoning me over. "Here he is now. Did you want to talk to him?"

She listened for a beat, then laughed. "Okay, I'll chat with you soon." She handed me the phone. "It's your sister."

I took the device wordlessly, staring at it for a second before raising it to my ear.

"Mari?"

"Hello, brother," she sounded choked, her voice heavy with emotion. "Or should I say, Uncle?"

I sucked in a breath. "You had the baby?"

"A little girl." Her voice broke. "We've named her Harpa."

I closed my eyes, grateful when Audrey's arms wrapped around my middle, holding me tight.

"And you're well?"

"We're both doing great. Farmer's ridiculously clucky, but we're muddling through."

I could just imagine the badass losing his brain over his daughter.

"I love you, sis."

"I love you too."

I heard her suck in a breath. "And you can thank Audrey for this. She sent a phone down with the last nomad crew. Apparently bribed them to get it to me."

I chuckled, turning to take my sneaky woman in my arms. She grinned up at me, her perfect face filled with joy.

"She'll get a proper thank you later."

Audrey winked.

A baby's cry sounded in the background.

"Is that?"

"Yep. That's your niece." Mari sighed. "I have to go. I think she's hungry."

"Of course. Kiss her for me."

"I will."

We signed off, and I placed the phone carefully on top of the transmitter.

Wrapping my arms around Audrey, I held her close. We were silent as I struggled to contain my raging emotions.

"Was it a good surprise?" she asked, finally breaking the silence.

"The best." I rested my chin on her head. "Thank you for this gift."

Her hand slipped down to pat my bottom. "You're welcome. Owning a genius has its perks."

I chuckled, rubbing my chin across her hair. "Mm? Such as?"

"Sex spreadsheets."

Laughing now, I pulled back to look down into her cheeky face. "I love you, Audrey."

She stood on tip-toe, her lips hovering above mine.

"I know."

We kissed, and everything in my world was perfect.

***

The Nameless Souls will continue with Pope.
Be sure to sign up to my newsletter for a bonus sneak peek!

You can continue the series, or start a new story from Evie Mitchell by checking them out on my website at www.EvieMitchell.com

*Enter the code **EBOOK10** to get 10% off your purchase from my website.*

ABOUT THE AUTHOR

Evie Mitchell is a thirty-something romance author (she/her/hers) living with disability. She believes in inclusion, accessibility, and fierce romance. Her loves include steamy romance novels, her husband, their THREE sausage dogs (heaven help her), and her ever-growing collection of book-related mugs.

As a woman with a diverse work history including in areas such as emergency response, event management, human rights, disability access, and security - her books are filled with true stories (bridezillas), worst-case scenarios (malfunctioning dresses), and her favourite tropes (one-bed).

Evie specialises in fiercely inclusive happily ever afters.

ALSO BY EVIE MITCHELL

Larsson Siblings Series

<u>Thunder Thighs</u>

<u>Clean Sweep</u>

<u>The X-list</u>

<u>Reality Check</u>

<u>The Christmas Contract</u>

Dogg Pack Books

<u>Puppy Love</u>

<u>Bad English</u>

<u>The Frock Up</u>

<u>Pier Pressure</u>

All Access Series

Knot My Type

Love Flushed

Capricorn Cove Series

<u>The Shake-Up</u>

<u>Double the D</u>

<u>Muffin Top</u>

<u>The Mrs. Clause</u>

<u>New Year Knew You</u>

<u>Double Breasted</u>

<u>As You Wish</u>

<u>You Sleigh Me</u>

<u>Resolution Revolution</u>

<u>Meat Load</u>

Nameless Souls MC Series

<u>Runner</u>

<u>Wrath</u>

<u>Ghost</u>

<u>Shield</u>

Elliot Security Series

<u>Rough Edge</u>

<u>Bleeding Edge</u>